*She gave the holy ones
the recompense of their labors,
conducted them by a wondrous road,
and became a shelter for them by day
and a starry flame by night.*
Wisdom 10:17

The intent and
purpose of this volume is to
give you faith, hope and inspiration.
Hopefully it will help bring peace and
tranquility into your life. May it be a
reminder of God's love, guidance
and His many blessings.

Our publications help to support our work
for needy children in over 130 countries
around the world. Through our programs,
thousands of children are fed, clothed,
educated, sheltered and given
the opportunity to live
decent lives.

Salesian Missions wishes to extend special thanks and gratitude to our generous poet friends and to the publishers who have given us permission to reprint material included in this book. Every effort has been made to give proper acknowledgments. Any omissions or errors are deeply regretted, and the publisher, upon notification, will be pleased to make the necessary corrections in subsequent editions.

Copyright ©2025 by Salesian Missions
2 Lefevre Lane, New Rochelle, NY 10801-5710 • Telephone: (914) 633-8344
Visit our website at: www.salesianmissions.org • Email: inspbks@salesianmissions.org

All Rights Reserved. ©72085E
Cover photo: ©BlueOrange Studio/Shutterstock.com

First Edition Printed in the U.S.A. by Concord Litho Group, Concord, NH 03301.

The Road Less Traveled

from the
Salesian Collection

Compiled and Edited by
Jennifer Grimaldi

Photo credits:
www.shutterstock.com

Dmitry Pistrov	Cliff LeSergent	Sunny studio	LanaG
Anastasiia Malinich	New Africa	NewJadsada	elod pali
Maya Kruchankova	locrifa	haveseen	gkordus
Judy Kennamer	ju_see	Andrew Mayovskyy	Elke Kohler
Daengpanya Atakorn	SoNelly	Evgeny Atamanenko	Feel good studio
PhotoJuli86	Rudmer Zwerver	katalinks	Patrick Poendl
TanKr	Team Toucan	Inga_Ivanova	MTetiana
Bachkova Natalia	Getman	George Sheldon	Roman Mikhailiuk
Iyon Design Graphic	KonstantinChristian	George Trumpeter	adamikarl
Andrea Kaulitzki	Javen	Cindy Goff	Andrii Spy_k
Leena Robinson	Ivonne Wierink	art180	Tatiana Buzmakova
gorillaimages	Ravshan Rakhimov	tilialucida	Shaiith
Nature's Charm	Patrick Jennings	Vova Shevchuk	Alina G
MarBom	FS Stock	Yadav Anil	Olha Rohulya
jakkapan	Alis Photo	kozirsky	
Ondrej Prosicky	LanaSweet	Veronika Galkina	
FamVeld	Nastyaofly	horsemen	

Contents

Morning Prayer 7

Meditation at Daybreak 9

I Never Borrow Trouble 11

Friendship Is a Journey 12

Friendship 15

Let the Lord's Spirit
    Guide You 17

A Friend Is Born 19

Dear Friendly God 21

Flowers From
    a Friend 23

Bravery 24

A Faithful Friend 27

There's Something
    About Evenings 28

Things I Love… 31

Good Morning, Lord 33

Times of Testing 35

The Pearl of Kindness 36

Stay Strong Amidst
    the Battle 39

Unwavering 41

A Prayer for Children 43

I Said a Prayer for You 45

'Til Our Eyes
    Meet Again 47

A Cherished Friend 49

Prayer for a Special
    Grandson 51

Summertime Is a
    Fun Time 52

Come Sail the Ship
    Called Friendship 55

I Thank God for
    This Day 57

All About Summer 58

Prayer for Friendship 61

Ode to Summer 63

Contents

Front Porch Memories 65	Bringing Out the Best of Winter 100
Falling Leaves 66	Lord God 103
Autumn Scene 67	Winter Wonder 104
A Harvest Prayer 69	A Crystal World 107
Autumn Walk 71	Winter Sunrise 108
Let Us Welcome Fall 73	Snowflakes 111
Autumn's Footsteps 75	A Meadow Filled With Snow 113
Autumn Pie 76	March Has Arrived 115
Golden Peace 79	Winter Is… 116
Awesome Wonder 80	Prayer of St. Francis of Assisi 119
Planting 83	The Glory of Winter 121
Autumn Sunrise 84	Wintertime Is a Time of Fun-Filled Magic 123
Dear Lord… 87	Altar Lamp 125
Life in Autumn 88	A World of White 127
Picturesque Beauty 91	Winter 128
Autumn 92	
Birds Take Flight 95	
September's Voice 97	
Winter Morning 98	

Morning Prayer

Dear God, thank You for the opportunity to see this new day. I pray for Your love and Your strength today. Please help me overcome any hurdles that may come my way. Please give me wisdom and guidance in everything that I do today so that my words and my actions will honor Your holy name. In Jesus' name, I pray, Amen

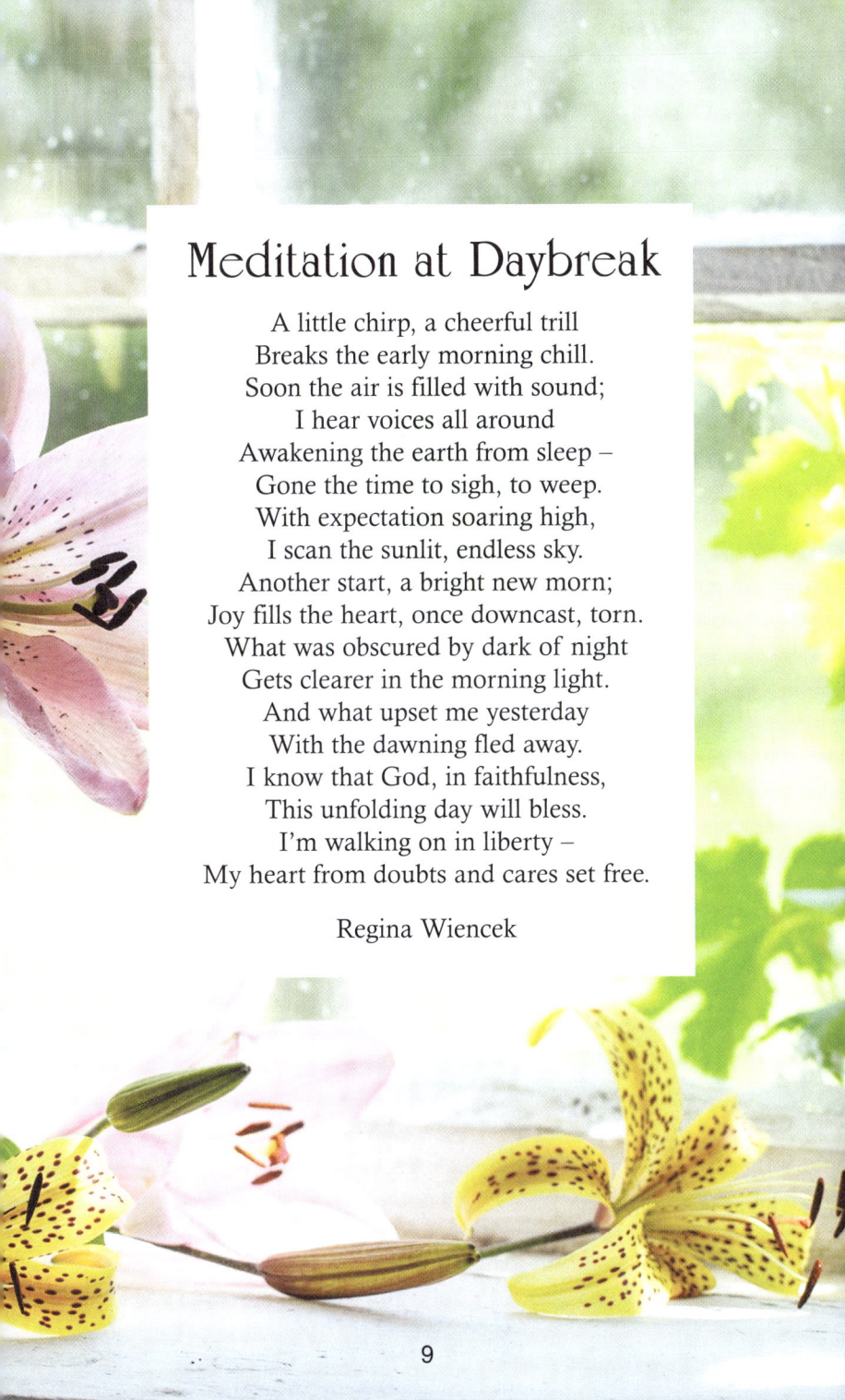

Meditation at Daybreak

A little chirp, a cheerful trill
Breaks the early morning chill.
Soon the air is filled with sound;
I hear voices all around
Awakening the earth from sleep –
Gone the time to sigh, to weep.
With expectation soaring high,
I scan the sunlit, endless sky.
Another start, a bright new morn;
Joy fills the heart, once downcast, torn.
What was obscured by dark of night
Gets clearer in the morning light.
And what upset me yesterday
With the dawning fled away.
I know that God, in faithfulness,
This unfolding day will bless.
I'm walking on in liberty –
My heart from doubts and cares set free.

Regina Wiencek

I Never Borrow Trouble

I never borrow trouble…
I just live from day to day,
Walking step-by-step with Jesus,
For I'm sure He knows the way.
Though tomorrow may bring problems,
Oftentimes of hurt and care,
I keep faith and find the answers
When I speak to God in prayer.

It's a waste to borrow trouble…
Seems that troubles come to all.
Life wasn't meant to be easy;
We must rise each time we fall.
In this great big world of beauty,
Every moment so worthwhile,
Never worry about tomorrow;
Just be happy – wear a smile.

Life is always worth the living…
Each today can be the best;
We've but to keep believing,
Then we'll meet the hardest test.
Just ahead the road is smoother,
Sunshine waits around the bend.
So don't ever borrow troubles;
Borrow laughter – be a friend.

Garnett Ann Schultz

Be on your guard, stand firm in the faith, be courageous, be strong.
1 Corinthians 16:13

Friendship Is a Journey

A friendship that is loyal and true
Is one you'll cherish throughout life –
It stands by you, steadfast in love and kindness
Amid hardships, good times and strife!
Hand in hand, together you'll journey
While traveling on smooth and rocky roads;
Whether neighborly near or miles afar,
In spirit, both carry a bit of the other's load.
A smile will brighten a friendship's path
And set the stars aglow;
Just a simple token that you care,
Causing a laugh or two to flow!

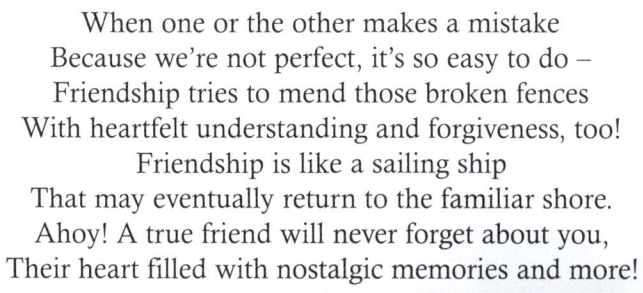

When one or the other makes a mistake
Because we're not perfect, it's so easy to do –
Friendship tries to mend those broken fences
With heartfelt understanding and forgiveness, too!
Friendship is like a sailing ship
That may eventually return to the familiar shore.
Ahoy! A true friend will never forget about you,
Their heart filled with nostalgic memories and more!

Linda C. Grazulis

Friendship

I'll say goodbye to you, my friend…
You're leaving quite an empty space;
A void that came so suddenly
As since our first embrace.

An embrace, and such a subtle one,
That saw us through the years;
I recall there were the hardships,
The rolling laughter – tears.

Now that you are leaving, friend,
I'll give our friendship a last embrace;
It won't be the same around here
And I hope you find a softer place.

I'll have to learn all over
What it means to lose a friend;
I hope to see you coming down the road again –
The longing will never end.

James Joseph Huesgen

*Happy is he who finds
a friend and he who
speaks to attentive ears.
Sirach 25:9*

Let the Lord's Spirit Guide You

Let the Lord's Spirit guide you
Through each hour, yes, every day;
He shall surely encourage,
Enlighten thee, on thy way,
Giving your heart grace and strength
For that which will come, or may,
Faithful, divine help anew –
One need simply only pray.

Steven Michael Schumacher

A Friend Is Born

Birthdays are so won rful,
For we celebrate the birth
Of those that are so dear to us,
A time of joy and mirth.
It's always such a happy time
For friends God's brought our way
That were born to cross our pathways
On a special pre-planned day.
He knew just what we needed,
The kind of friend for us;
Someone just right to be with
That we could love and trust.
And as years pass by,
We form an even closer bond;
As we share our joys and sorrows,
We become of each more fond.
So I thank the Lord for birthdays,
For each birth brings forth a friend
That's especially meant for someone
To be a friend right to the end.
He plans it all ahead of time,
This God that loves and cares;
A birthday means a friend is born
For someone soon to share.

Helen Gleason

Dear Friendly God

Lord God of love and friendship,
Thank You that You're our Friend.
We praise You for this friendship
That You give without an end.
Your friendship is delightful.
Your friendship we do seek.
Please accept the friendship
Of the prideful turning meek.
Let us walk with You, dear Lord.
Hold our hands, our dearest Friend.
We seek You to walk beside us
When we go around every bend.

Amen

Carol Zileski

Flowers From a Friend

I love every plant and flower
In the gardens I tend,
For most of them are special gifts
I received from a friend.
Every blossom's a reminder
Of those who came my way
To share a cup of kindness
And brighten up my day.

Some came from seeds or cuttings
Handed down through the years
To share with friends and loved ones
Through laughter and the tears.
Love blossoms in my gardens
With every seed I sow,
And sweet memories surround me
That set my heart aglow.

My flowers represent my friends,
Even those who live apart,
For remembrance is a garden
That blossoms in the heart.
My spirits are lifted higher
With each bouquet I send,
For nothing says, "I love you,"
Like flowers from a friend.

Clay Harrison

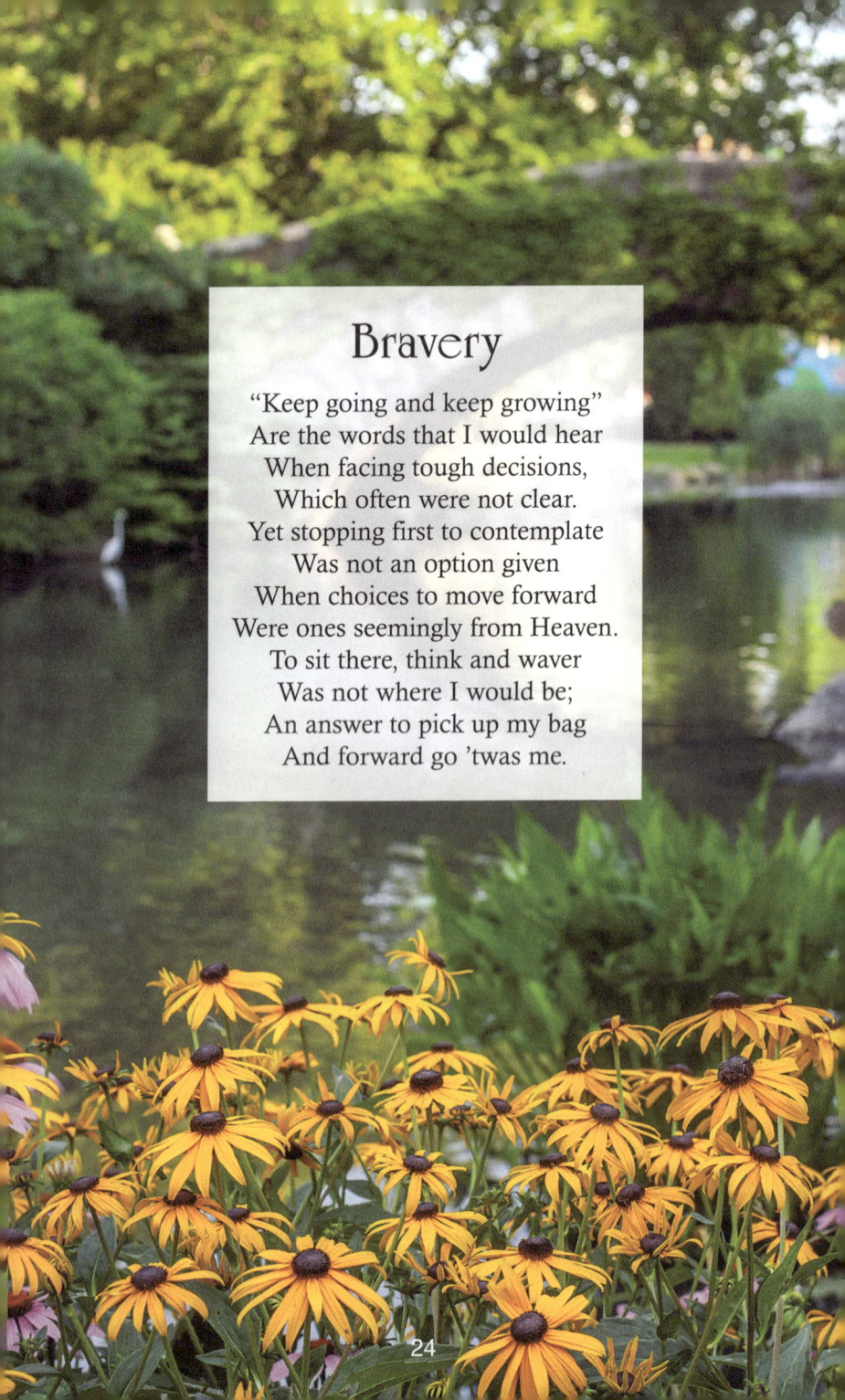

Bravery

"Keep going and keep growing"
Are the words that I would hear
When facing tough decisions,
Which often were not clear.
Yet stopping first to contemplate
Was not an option given
When choices to move forward
Were ones seemingly from Heaven.
To sit there, think and waver
Was not where I would be;
An answer to pick up my bag
And forward go 'twas me.

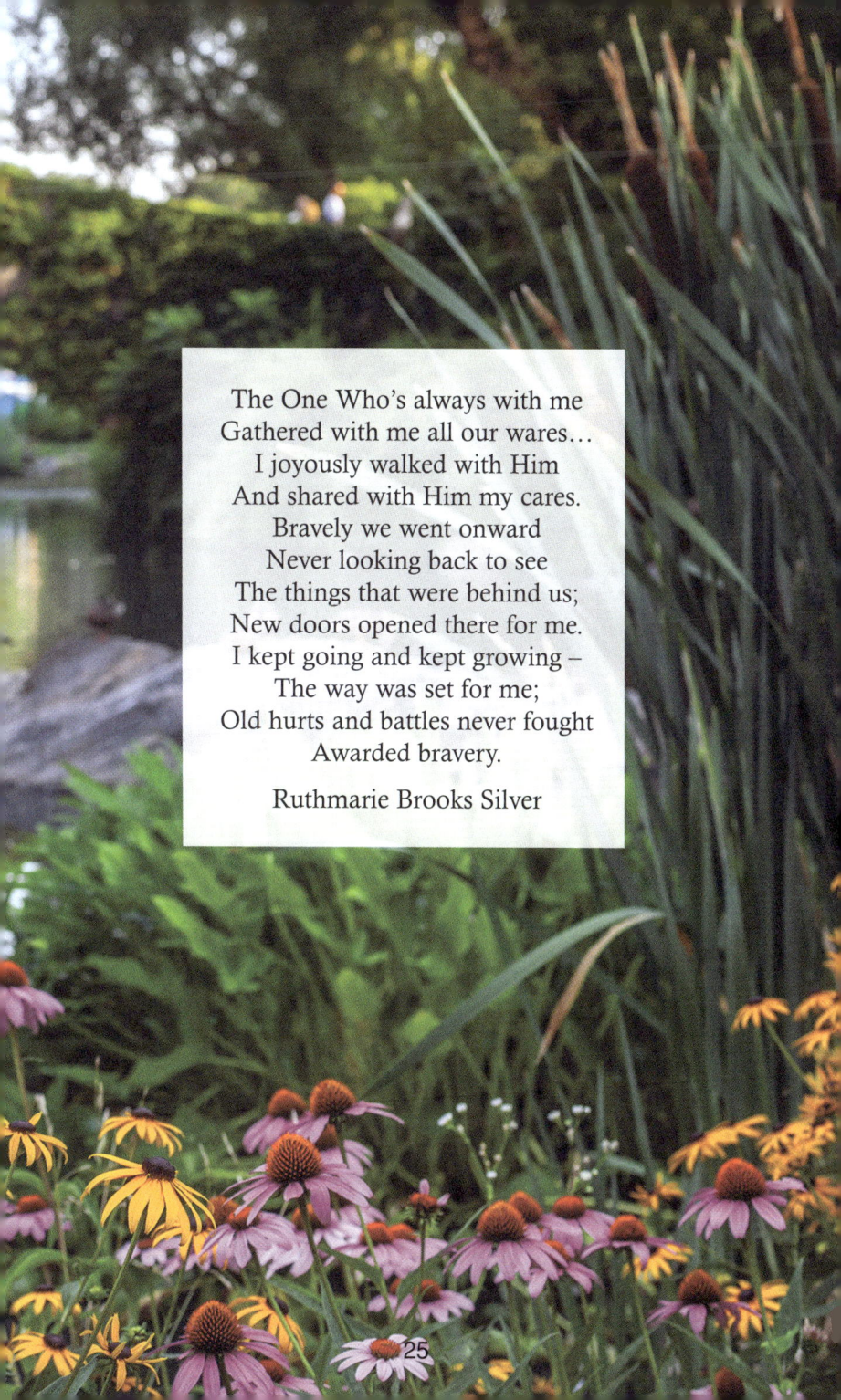

The One Who's always with me
Gathered with me all our wares…
I joyously walked with Him
And shared with Him my cares.
Bravely we went onward
Never looking back to see
The things that were behind us;
New doors opened there for me.
I kept going and kept growing –
The way was set for me;
Old hurts and battles never fought
Awarded bravery.

Ruthmarie Brooks Silver

A Faithful Friend

Sometimes loneliness overwhelms me,
Like a black cloud on a stormy day.
That's when I long for the love of a friend
To come and help chase the gloom away.

A friend, it seems, knows what to say,
With words of comfort to give me hope.
Sometimes the presence of a faithful friend
Is all I need to help me cope.

Sometimes my mood is sad and gloomy
And I think that no one cares.
It is then God sends a faithful friend…
His promised answer to my prayers.

A sincere hug can say so much,
More than words in its own way.
Just knowing my friend is near…
Can say much more than words can say.

A faithful friend knows when to listen,
As sometimes words can get in the way.
A friend will lend a shoulder to lean on…
Our God is like that every day.

Charles Clevenger

There's Something About Evenings

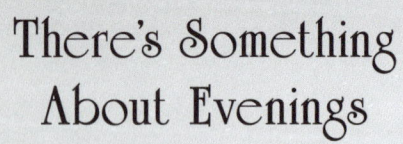

There's something about evenings
When everything is still;
I hear the children's laughter
All the way across the hill.
The birds have ceased their singing,
Wings flutter as they fly;
Soon the sun will slowly set,
So the moon can light the sky.
The air is growing cooler,
The heat of day is faint,
And the glory of the sunset
Is one I wish that I could paint.
I see God winking at me
As the first stars greet the night;
There's something about evenings…
I hear God whisper, "All is right."

Margie Rieske

Things I Love...

I love each passing moment,
I love a sunny sky,
I love a purple necklace
And babies when they cry...

I love a friendly handshake,
I love a happy smile,
I love a fragrant flower
And things that are worthwhile...

I love a pretty poem,
I love a blue-green sea,
I love a frisky kitty,
And I love them 'cause they're free...

I love a charming person,
I love a rocking chair,
I love the smell of coffee,
And I love a simple prayer...

I love to watch the lightning,
I love the morning dew,
But more than all these blessings,
I love good friends like you!

Hope C. Oberhelman

*For the house of the Lord,
our God, I pray, "May
blessings be yours."
Psalm 122:9*

Good Morning, Lord

Here I sit again
In my favorite chair,
With a view of the skies
And trees, black and bare.

Cold rain hits the windows.
No birdsong I hear.
Gray clouds drift by slowly;
There is nothing to cheer.

But sweet peace surrounds me,
Here in my old home.
My refuge, my shelter;
Let stormy winds roam.

I am contented,
For I've found a friend
Who is always with me
To uplift and defend.

Regina Wiencek

Times of Testing

When you're facing difficulties,
It is easy to complain.
Be at peace, the tide is turning;
Before long, you'll smile again.
Days of turmoil, doubts and setbacks,
You endure as time goes by.
God directs you every footstep;
There's no need to question why –
Why the problems I am facing,
And the joyful days so few?
Maybe God, in His own timing,
Introduces something new.
He prepares His chosen vessels
For the task He has in mind.
There's a purpose for each person;
We are all one of a kind.

Regina Wiencek

*How great are Your works,
Lord! How profound
Your purpose!
Psalm 92:6*

The Pearl of Kindness

God blessed you with such kindness, friend;
A pearl of unequaled price –
You go out of your way to help me,
And only your best will suffice.

And I thank you for loving and helping me;
I'm sustained by knowing you care –
The bond that is so strong between us
Is one blessed by God… and so rare.

Dear Lord, I praise You for my friend!
She means just the world to me –
And if I could make one request,
It's that You would hear my plea…

To bless her and those in her family
And to keep them close to Your heart;
Bless all their present endeavors
And those You are still to impart.

For no one but You, Lord, can do this,
And You will if I "trust and obey" –
Now I pray that she hears with her heart
These next few words I have to say…

Dear Friend, I love you completely!
Keep doing what you do in love –
Polish the gem that God gave you,
And He'll bless you with joy from above.

    Denise A. DeWald

Stay Strong Amidst the Battle

Life is hard, and days get weary.
Battles come, and storm clouds grow.
Rainbows come after the rainstorms.
Of this one thing, I know.

Put your sighing into worship.
Turn your fear into faith.
Don't let anxiety control your thinking.
But remember God's awesome grace.

God is with you in the battle
When it rages all around.
He is faithful to His children.
His love, it knows no bounds.

One day, our battles are over.
The struggles all will cease.
We'll be on our way to Heaven
Where there's endless joy and peace.

Mary Ann Jameson

*Be strong and take heart, all you who hope in the Lord.
Psalm 31:25*

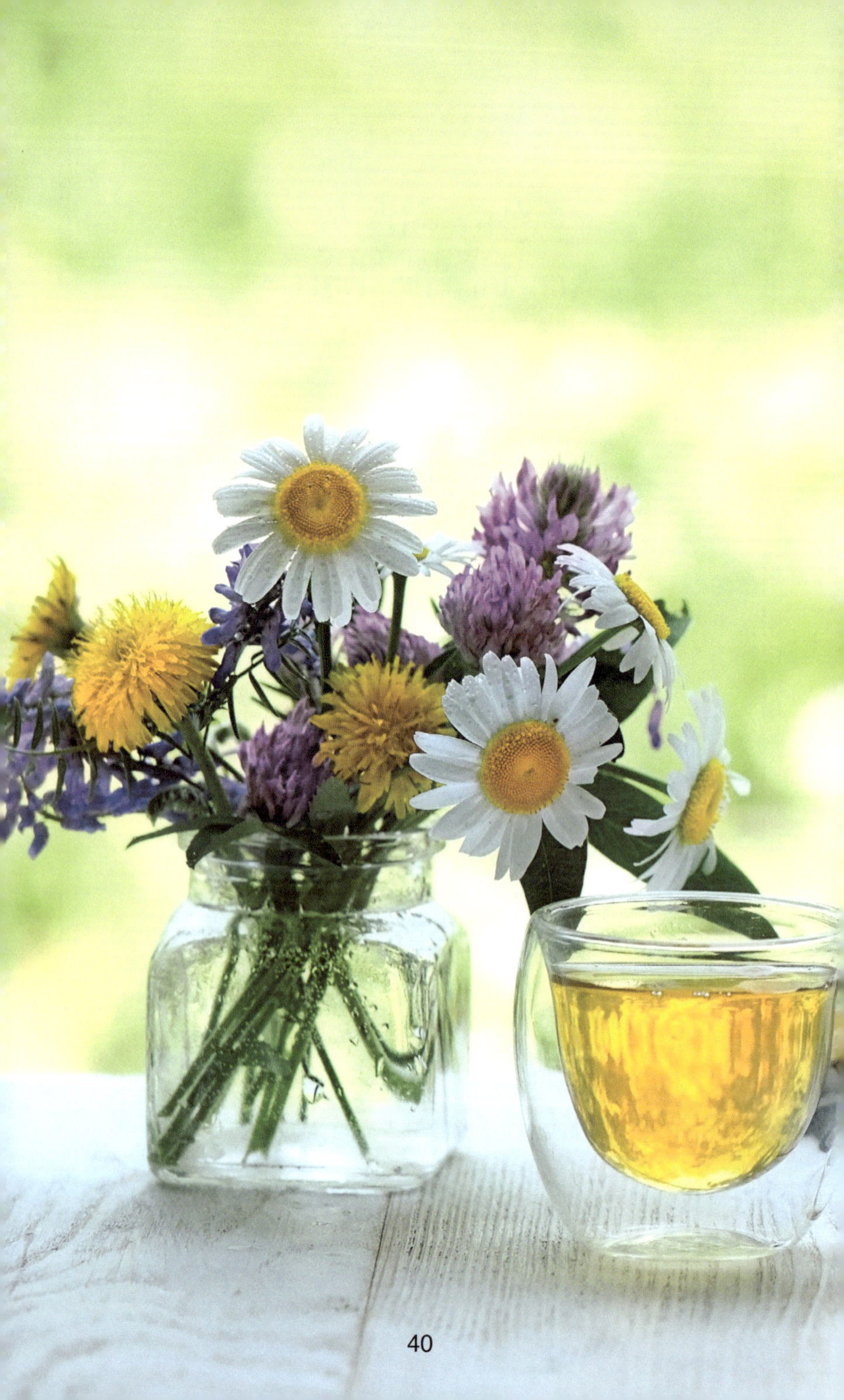

Unwavering

Consider Christ when in despair,
When you're in pain or broken down.
He will reveal to you, He cares;
Beyond all reason, comfort is found.

Offer Him the power as you look up;
Pray for compliance and hear His call.
Deliver praise as He fills your cup;
Grasp… He doesn't want you to fall.

His conviction instead is of good,
By His love for you and all creation;
Listen to His Word as you should,
And thank Him for your salvation.

Sheila Hayes Boucher

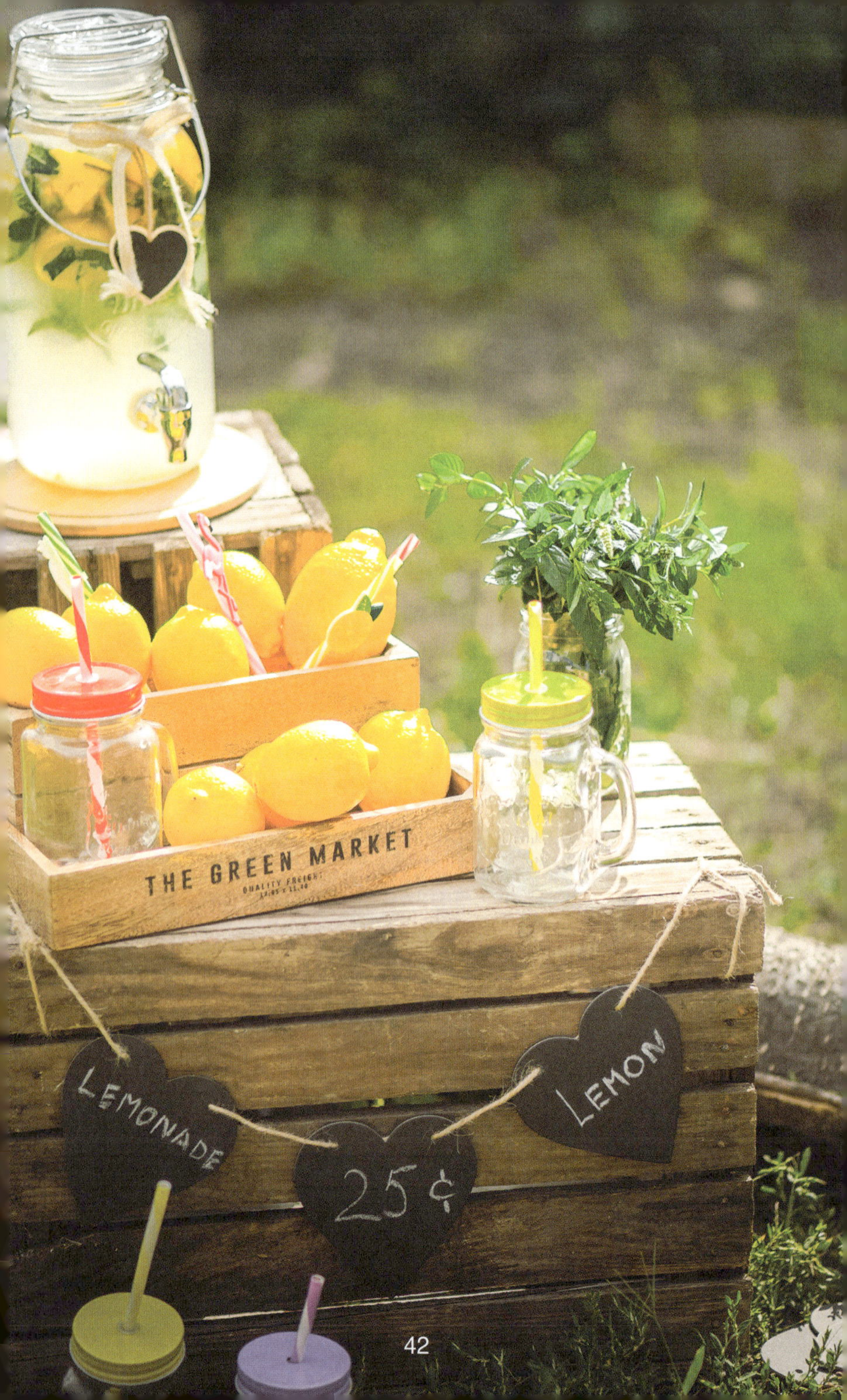
THE GREEN MARKET
LEMONADE
25¢
LEMON

A Prayer for Children

*God our Father, You have blessed us
with the gift of children;
thank You for these precious gems
that fill our house.
Their laughter gives us
joy and brightens our lives.
They are the expressions of Your
presence in our home.
Their growth shows
the mysteries of Your love.
May they experience Your loving
presence, advance in wisdom
and grow in Your love.
Our children's future is in
Your hand, and yet we have our own
role to play in shaping that future.
Help us to be true to our responsibility
so that we may assist
them in responding to Your
graces and thus to become
what we want them to be.
Amen*

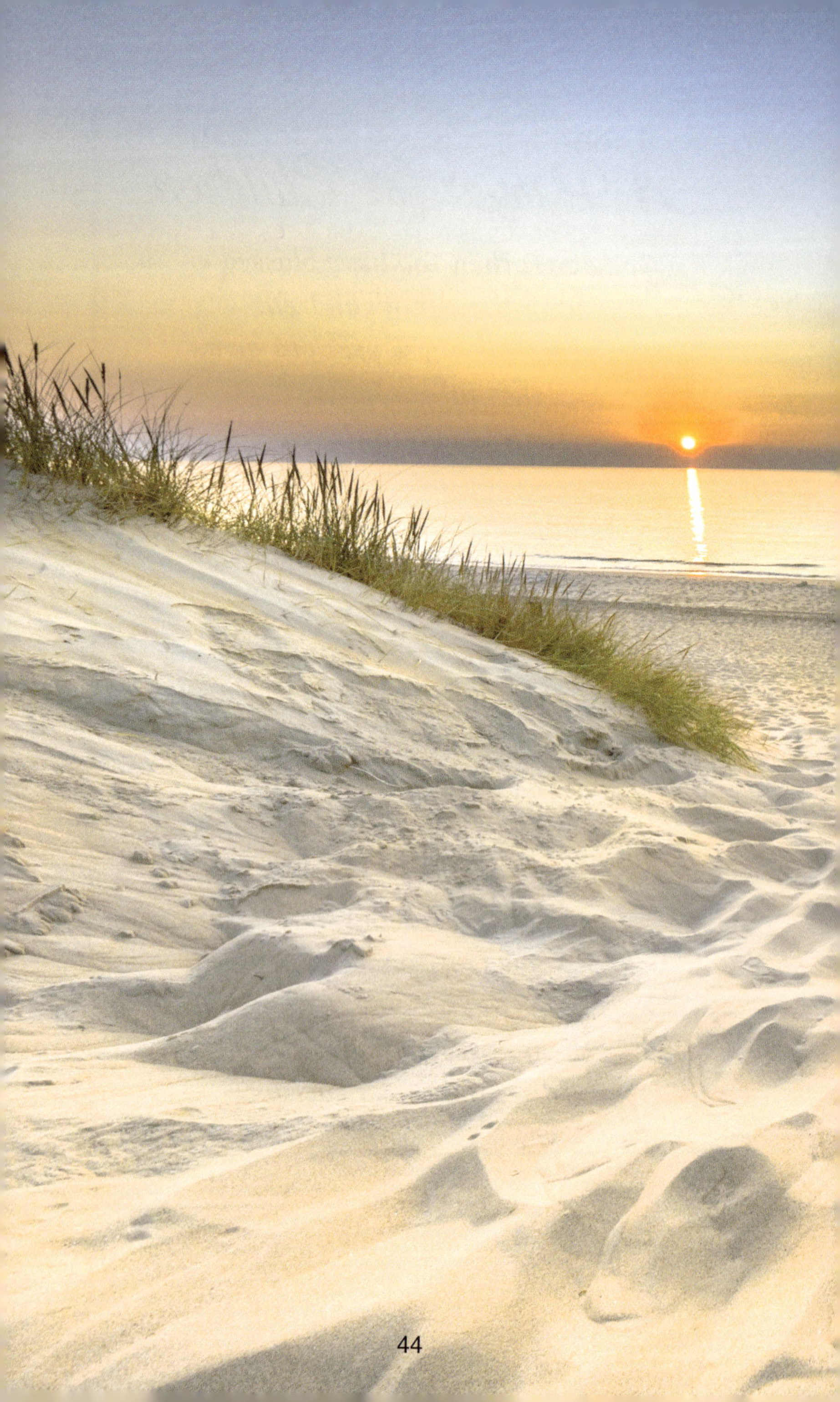

I Said a Prayer for You

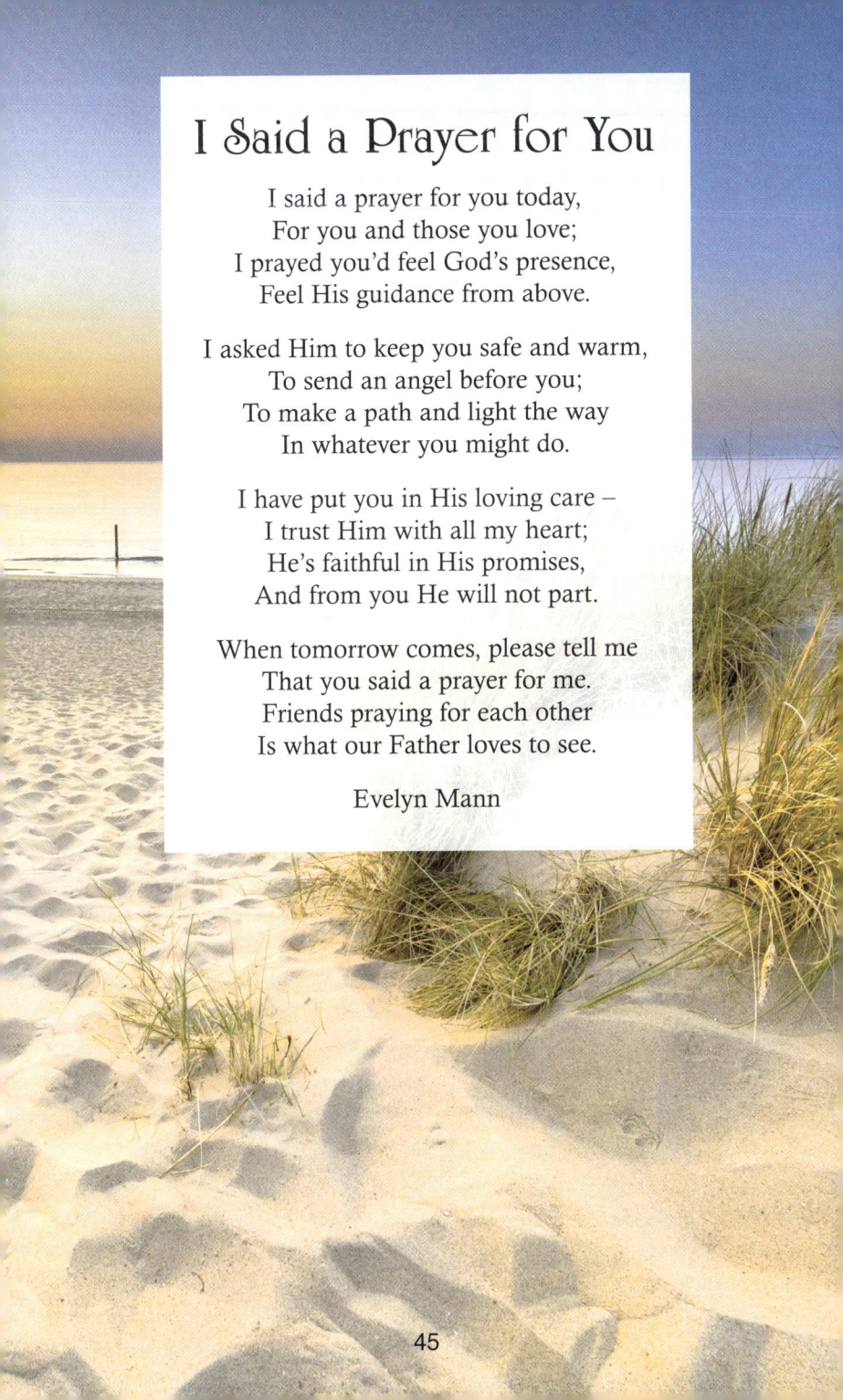

I said a prayer for you today,
For you and those you love;
I prayed you'd feel God's presence,
Feel His guidance from above.

I asked Him to keep you safe and warm,
To send an angel before you;
To make a path and light the way
In whatever you might do.

I have put you in His loving care –
I trust Him with all my heart;
He's faithful in His promises,
And from you He will not part.

When tomorrow comes, please tell me
That you said a prayer for me.
Friends praying for each other
Is what our Father loves to see.

Evelyn Mann

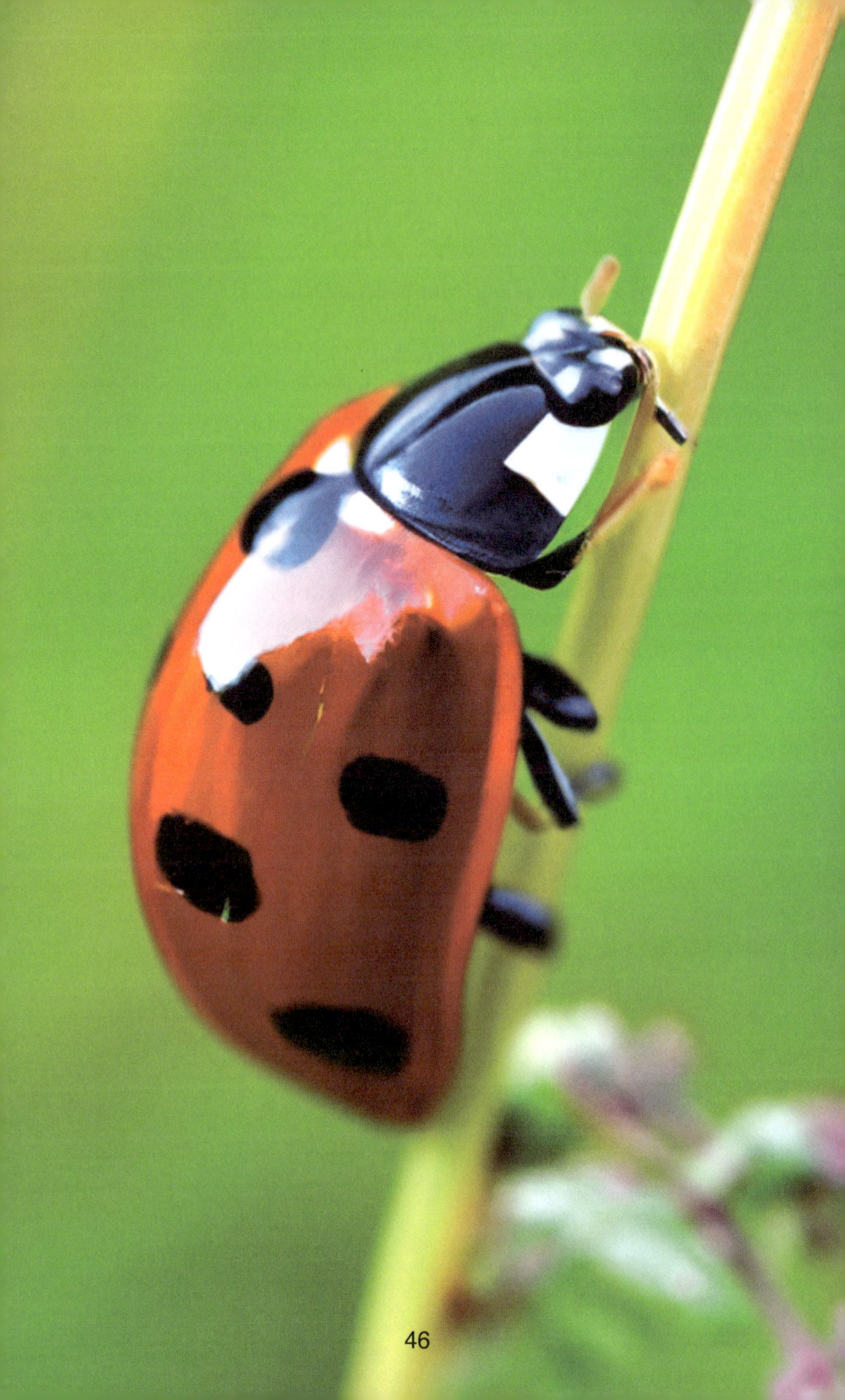

'Til Our Eyes Meet Again

'Til our eyes meet again,
May you fare well,
And peace be yours
And in you dwell.

'Til our eyes meet again,
May God's blessing be yours,
And His Light guide you 'til
Your return be sure.

'Til our eyes meet again,
May God be with you,
And good fortune attend
All that you do.

'Til our eyes meet again,
Though we know not when,
I'll be looking for you –
Fare thee well 'til then.

Helen Gleason

Then we who are alive, who are left, will be caught up together with them in the clouds to meet the Lord in the air. Thus we shall always be with the Lord.
1 Thessalonians 4:17

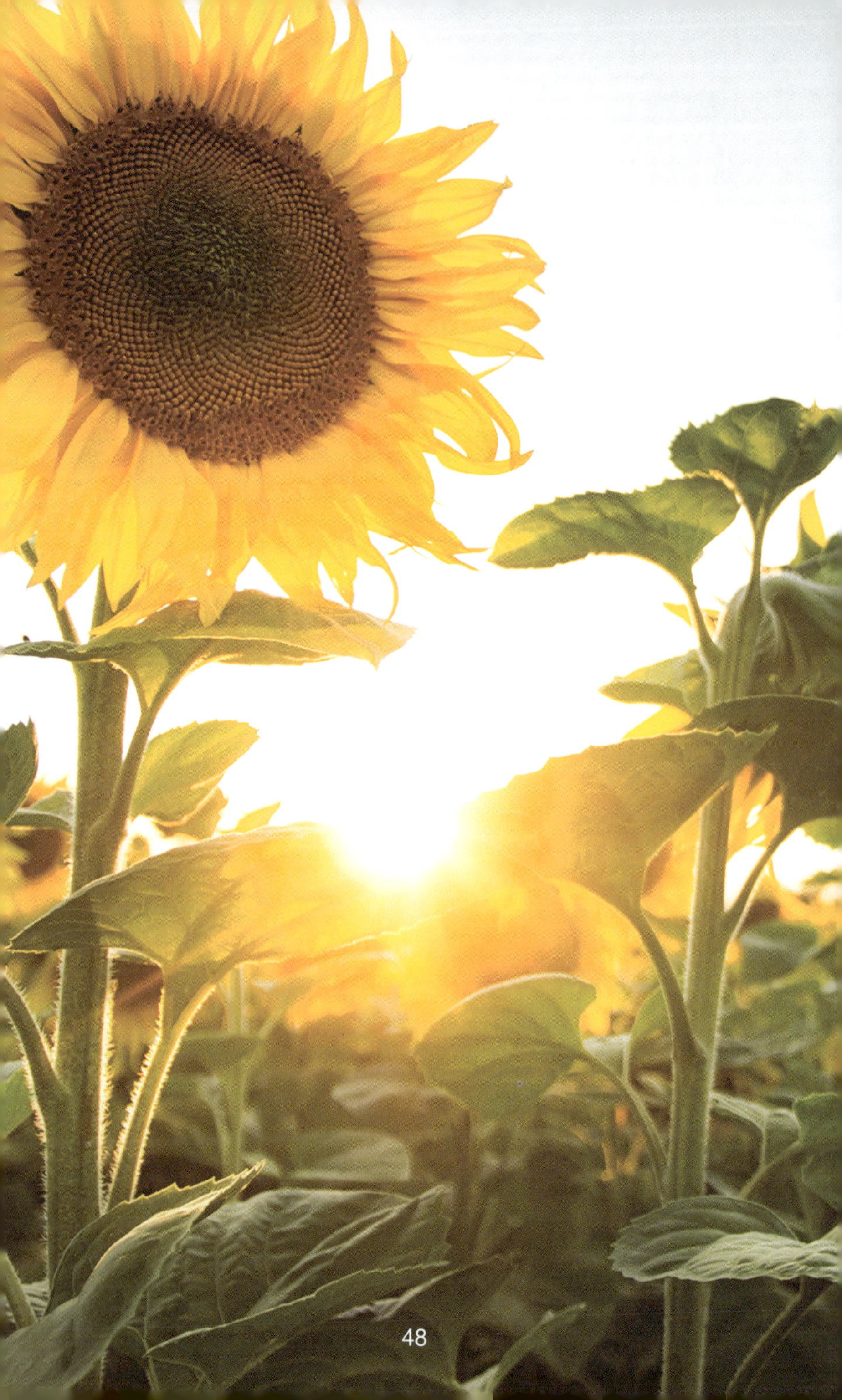

A Cherished Friend

The distant miles that lie between,
With fields, valleys, mountains and streams,
All seem to me so very small
When I look and see God's hand in it all.
For a cherished friend we hold in our heart
When so many miles keep us far apart;
I think that God must want it that way,
Least we should forget from day to day
To hold each other in high esteem,
And lose the vision of a beautiful dream.
But someday soon we too shall be
With Jesus our Lord in reality.

Gertrude McKenzie

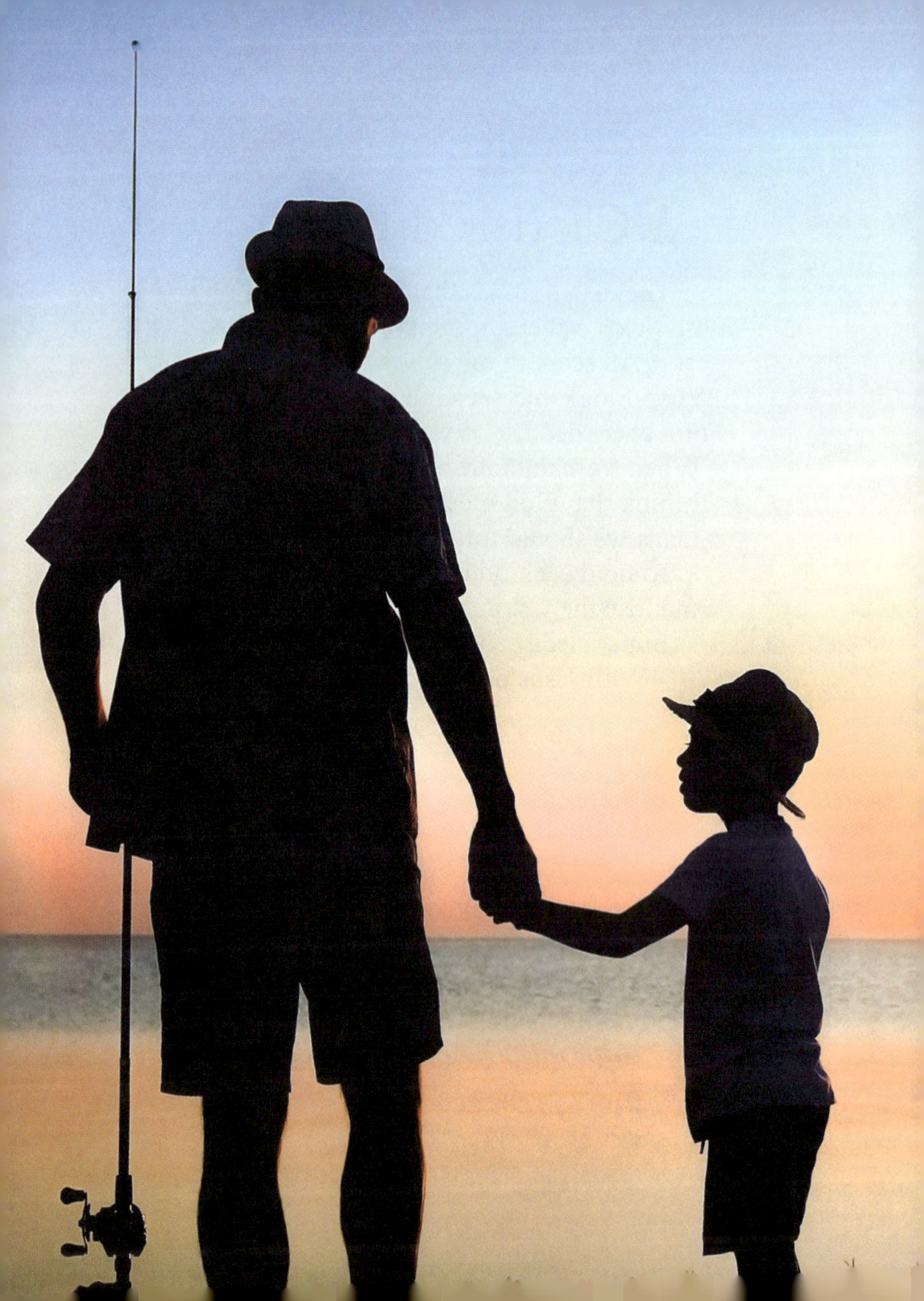

Prayer for a Special Grandson

*I pray for my grandson,
that he may be blessed
with good health,
happiness and wisdom.
Please guide him and protect him
as he navigates through life's journey.
Grant him the strength to
overcome challenges and the courage
to pursue his dreams.
May he be surrounded by love,
support and positive influences.
Help me be a source of guidance
and inspiration for him,
and may he always feel
Your presence in his life.*
Amen

Summertime Is a Fun Time

Summertime is a fun time
For hungry ants and picnics in the park,
The sounds of children's laughter,
Watching fireflies blink in the dark.
It's running through a grassy meadow
Without shoes upon your feet,
Jumping on a haystack,
Rows and rows of swaying wheat.
Going on vacation –
Humming Summer songs,
Leaping with the ocean waves,
Feeling you belong.
Summertime is a fun time –
Free of the Winter's chill;
God created this season for adventure,
So get out and experience the thrill.

Linda C. Grazulis

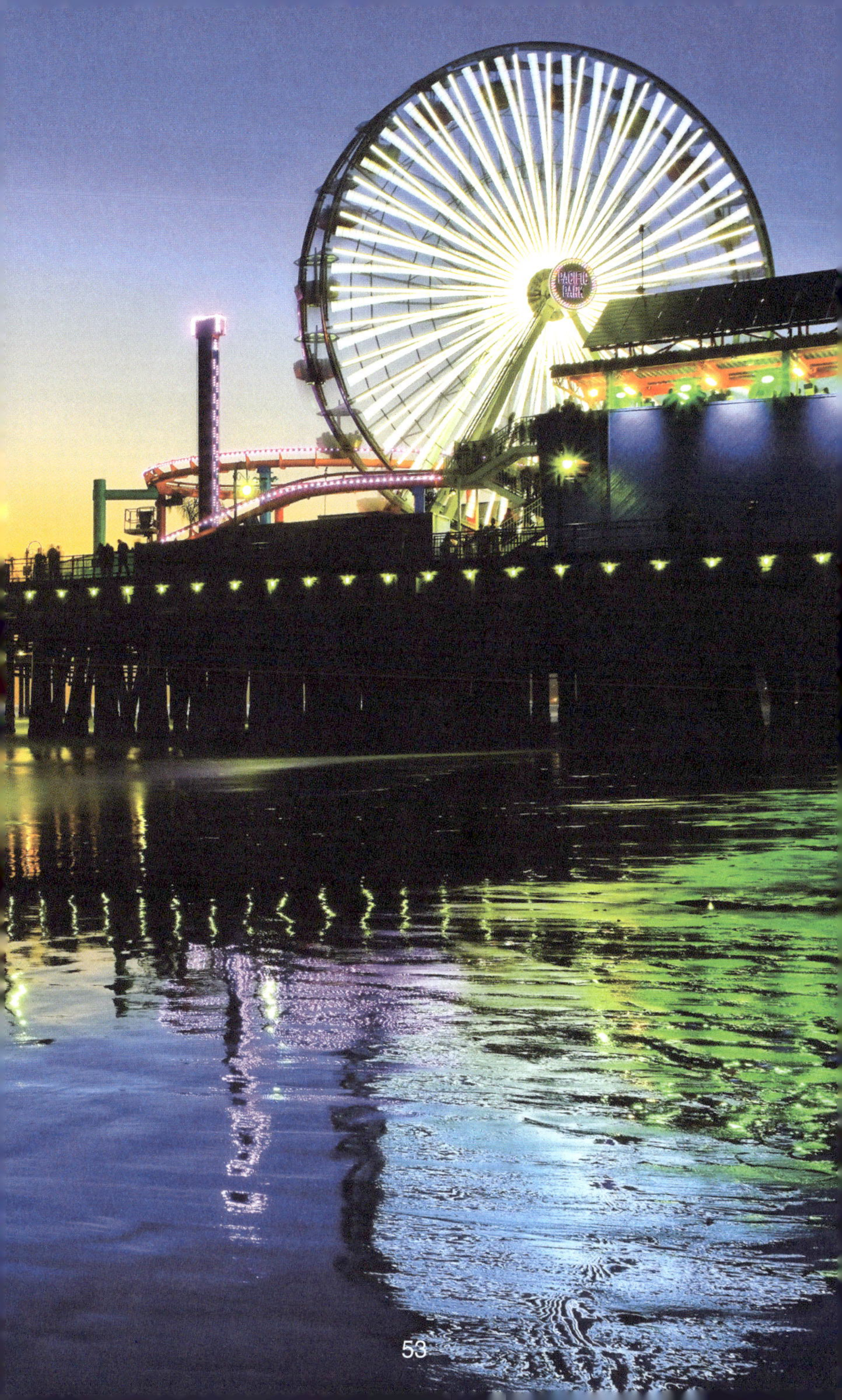
PACIFIC
PARK

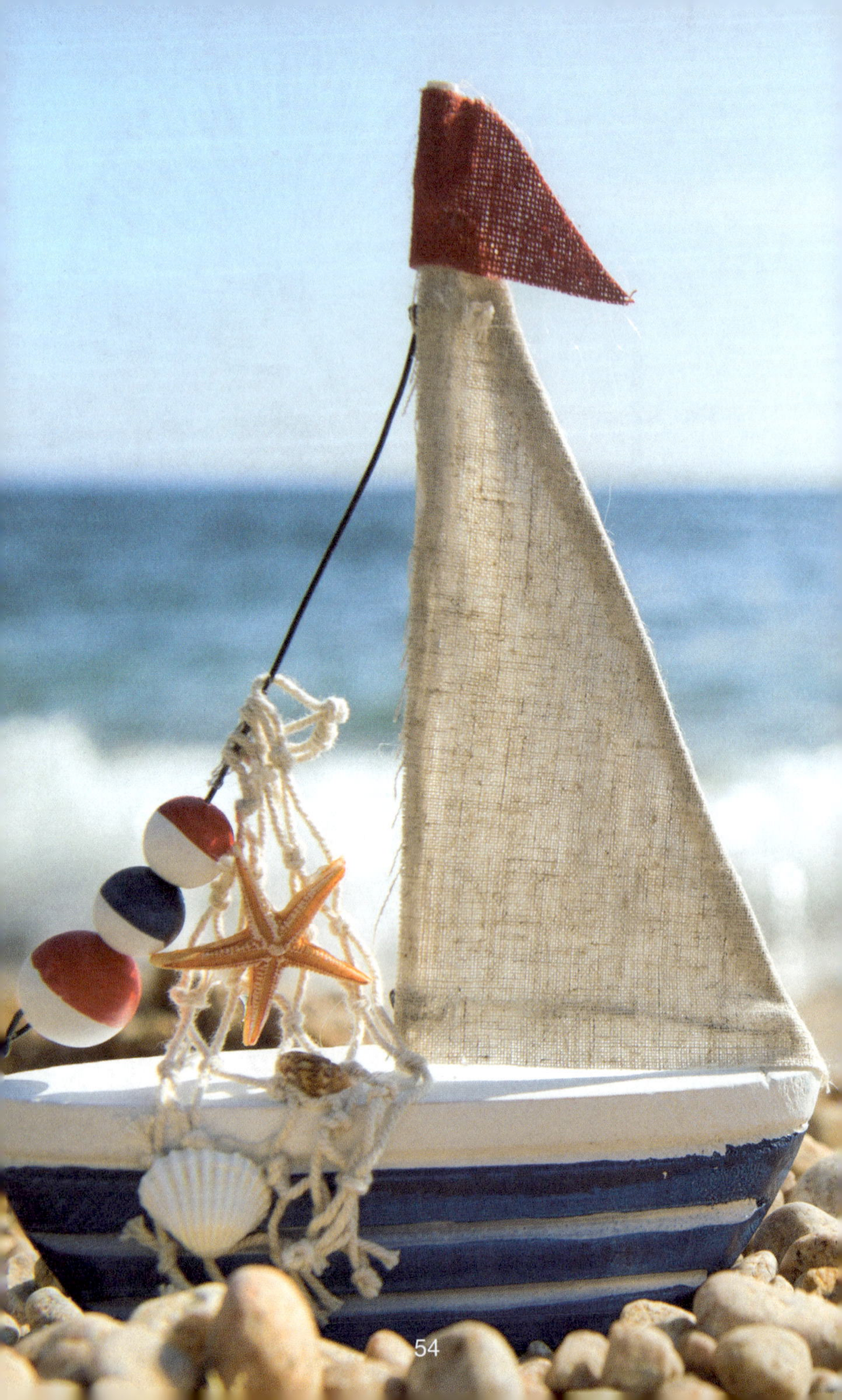

Come Sail the Ship Called Friendship

Come aboard the ship called friendship
Where camaraderie dwells and thrives;
It's such a pleasure to share with others –
Praise God, you're pleased to be alive!
Open the door; you're so welcome inside
As we chuckle and giggle and more…
Telling silly jokes and tales of fun,
So much humor and stories galore.
"The more the merrier," we've often heard
As we drift along life's sea.
Don't be shy, timid, or an island –
Let's get together and heartily clang our mugs of tea.
Take a risk to open your heart –
Who knows, maybe disappointed you won't be.
When aboard this ship called friendship,
You may find a connection and solely agree.
Slip right on in and join the crew
Of others, perhaps, just like you,
Who are lonely or bored, seeking someone
Who also longs for similar hobbies, something to do.
Life is just a journey… why travel alone
When the world is filled with friends?
One never knows whom God has created
To be the special one your broken heart to mend.

Linda C. Grazulis

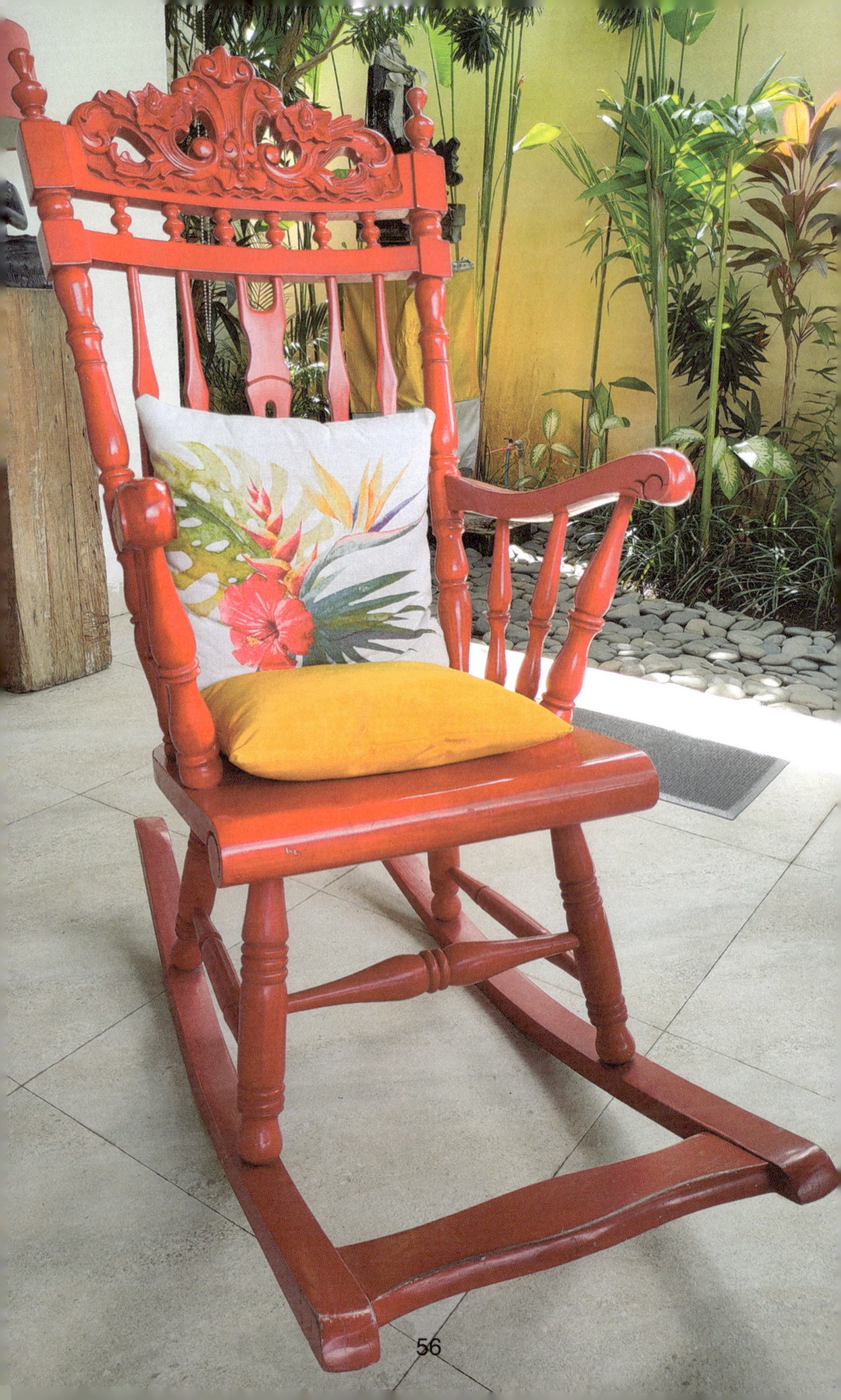

I Thank God for This Day

Buttercups cover the meadow;
They are dancing in the wind.
Might be because the sunbeams
Have filled their blossoms to the brim.
As far as my eyes see,
Distant daisies bend and sway.
Lucky me to be outdoors
On this late Summer day.
The butterflies have landed
On the cone flowers near the woods.
The busy bees are buzzing too,
Their soft humming sounds quite good.
Oh the sights and sounds of Summer,
Like the rippling of the stream;
I sit beside the water
On rock benches to daydream.
Nature's beauty is overwhelming;
It always takes my breath away.
Beneath a sky of brilliant blue,
I thank God for this day!

Margie Rieske

All About Summer

The hills are green… it's Summer –
The sun is warm and bright;
And everyone is loving it
From morning until night.
The clouds are giant whiteness
Suspended in the blue;
And creatures with a freeness
Roam where grass is new.
All birds soar ever upward –
Beyond the moving leaves
That reach for Summer's Heaven
Whenever there is breeze.

Beside the country pathways,
Daisies bend and sway;
And morning glories hug the fences,
Crossing in their way.
No one could wish for Winter
When Summer is so grand,
As Nature's colors and aromas
Dance across the land.

Joan Stephen

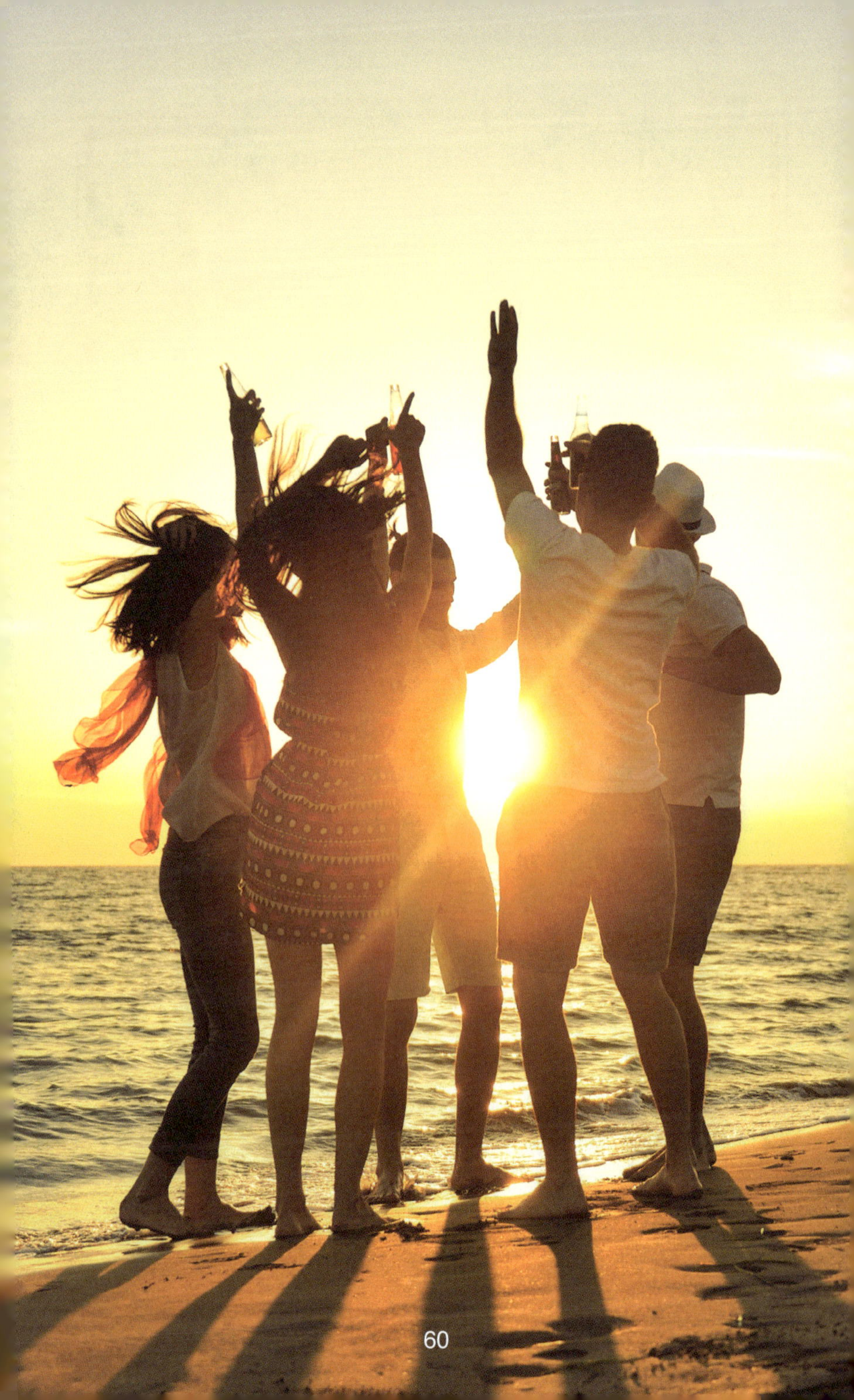

Prayer for Friendship

*You have blessed us, O God,
with the gift of friendship,
the bonding of persons
in a circle of love.
We thank You for such a blessing:
for friends who love us,
who share our sorrows,
who laugh with us in celebration,
who bear our pain,
who need us as we need them,
who hold us when words fail,
and who give us the freedom
to be ourselves.
Bless our friends with health,
wholeness, life and love.*
Amen

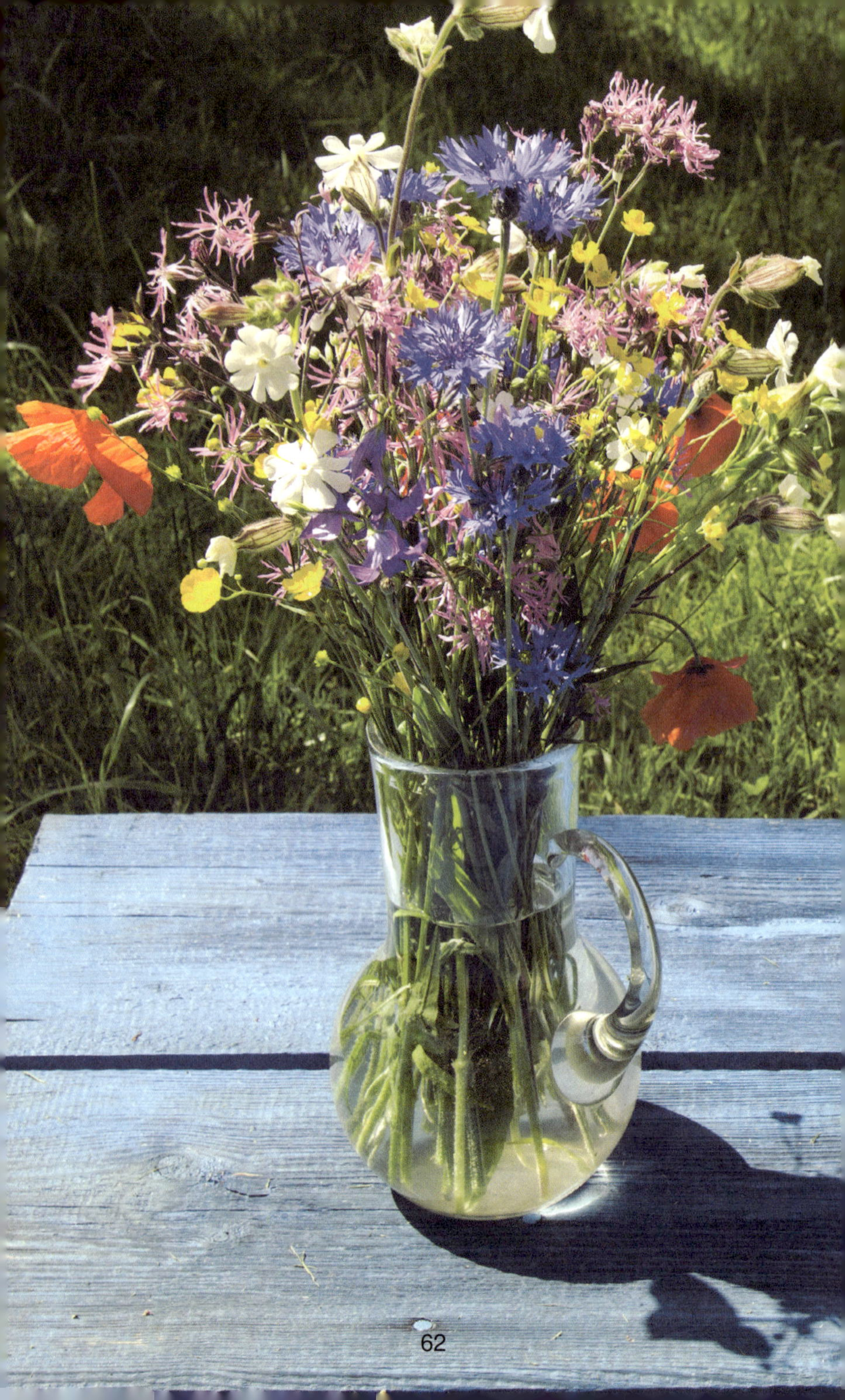

Ode to Summer

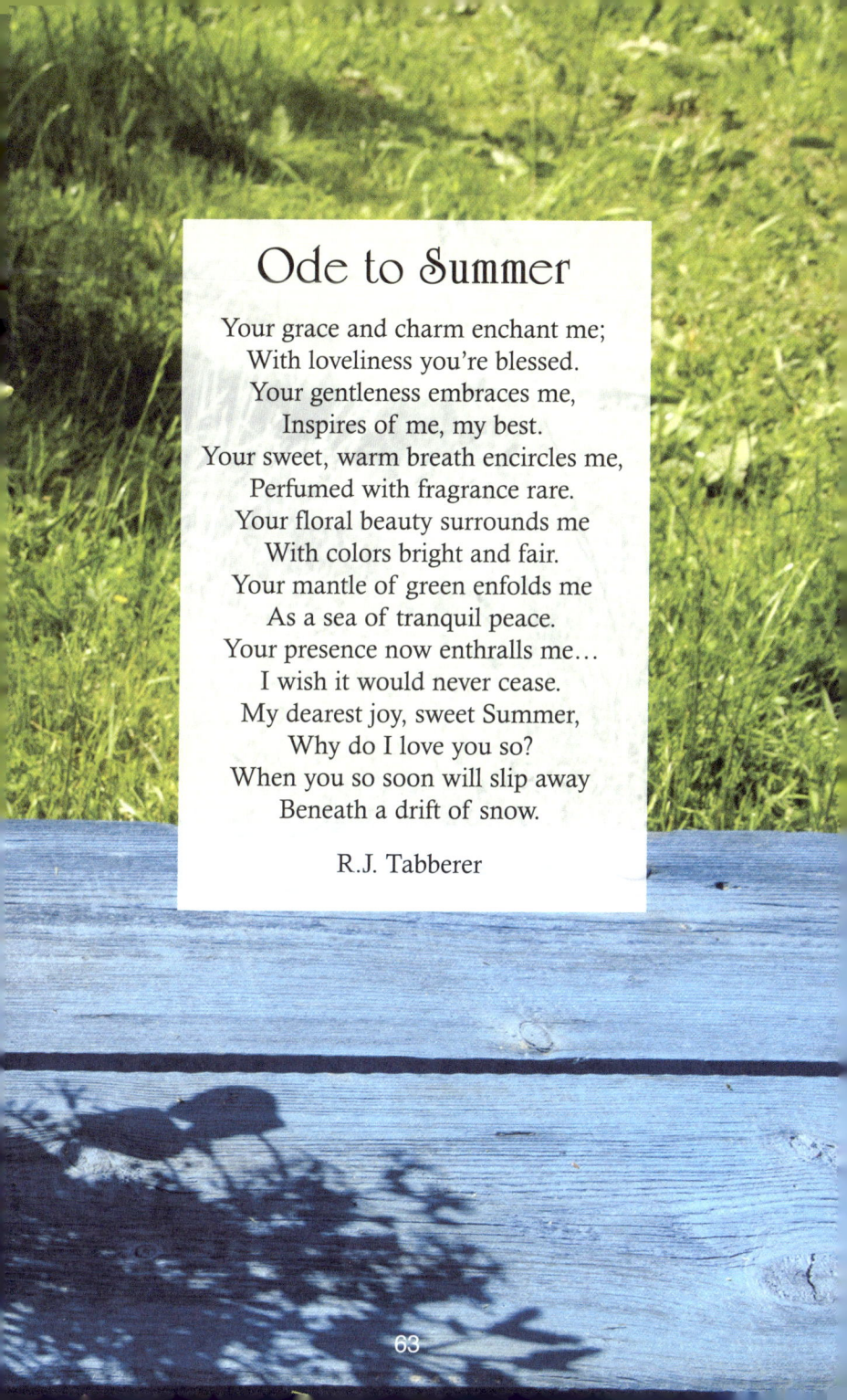

Your grace and charm enchant me;
With loveliness you're blessed.
Your gentleness embraces me,
Inspires of me, my best.
Your sweet, warm breath encircles me,
Perfumed with fragrance rare.
Your floral beauty surrounds me
With colors bright and fair.
Your mantle of green enfolds me
As a sea of tranquil peace.
Your presence now enthralls me…
I wish it would never cease.
My dearest joy, sweet Summer,
Why do I love you so?
When you so soon will slip away
Beneath a drift of snow.

R.J. Tabberer

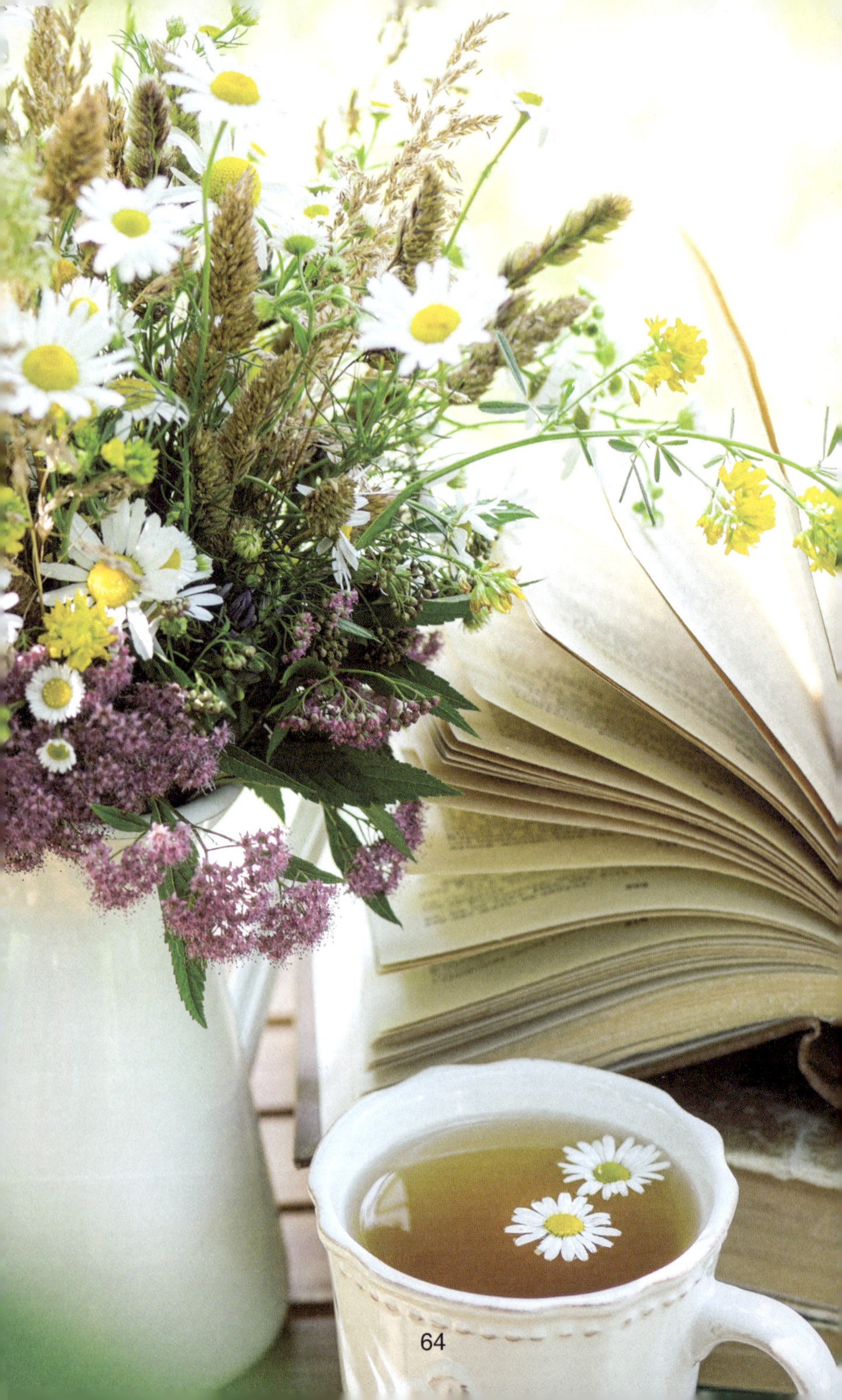

Front Porch Memories

I love to think of days gone by,
Of my old neighborhood;
It was so alive and carefree,
And our lives were good.

We had such caring neighbors,
Who loved us and it showed;
Not just with smiles and laughter,
But they helped us bear our load.

We all just felt like family,
All doors were open wide;
The "welcome" mat was always out,
Bidding, "come inside."

I loved those precious people,
They filled my life with joy.
The richness that they added,
Nothing can destroy.

When Summer winds begin to blow,
I sit on my porch swing
And reminisce of days gone by –
Oh, what happiness it brings.

Mary Ann Jameson

*Welcome one another, then,
as Christ welcomed you,
for the glory of God.
Romans 15:7*

Falling Leaves

Down come the leaves, bright yellow and red,
Settling soon in a snug Winter bed,
Floating upon the wings of the breeze,
Twisting and turning with delicate ease.

I sit by the window, entranced by the sight,
And follow the course of beauty in flight,
To unite in array on grass that's still green –
No artist could paint a more beautiful scene.

Lester E. Bartholomew

Autumn Scene

Each Autumn day brings joy untold
In a Fall display of colors bold;
My heart is filled with joy serene,
For God's hand touched this Autumn scene.

Nora M. Bozeman

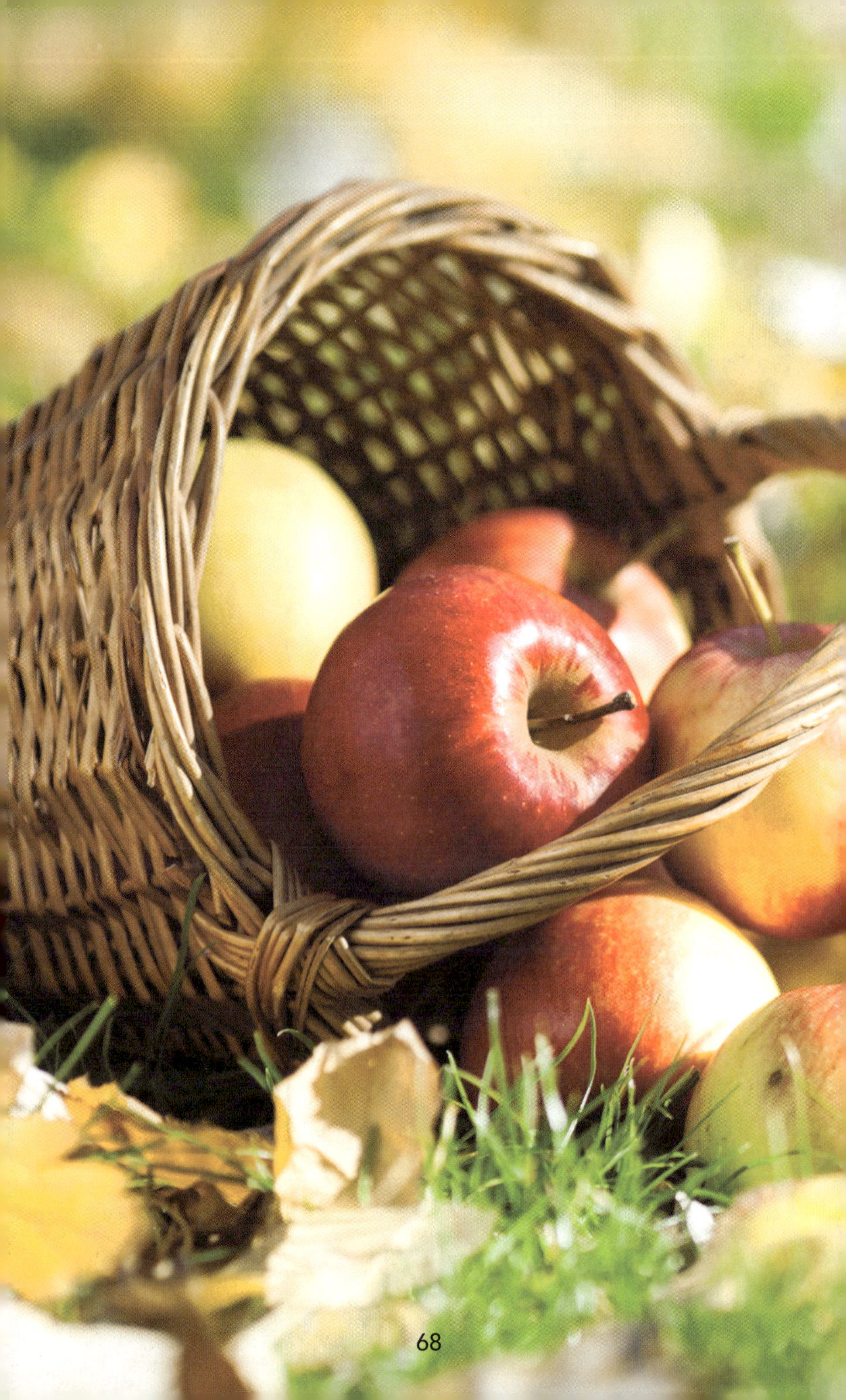

A Harvest Prayer

*I give thanks to You, Lord over all the earth.
I give thanks to You, Savior,
Redeemer, Forgiver of my sins.
I give thanks to You Who made
the sun and rain. I give thanks to You
for new growth that rises from fertile land.
I give thanks to You for harvests and grain,
for nourishing bread. I give thanks to You
for fruit and vegetables, full of goodness.
I give thanks to You for fresh milk
and eggs just laid. I give thanks to You
for the hearty and healthy provision
of meat and fish. I give thanks
to You for all Your great bounty.
Surely, we taste Your goodness
today with truly thankful hearts.*

Amen

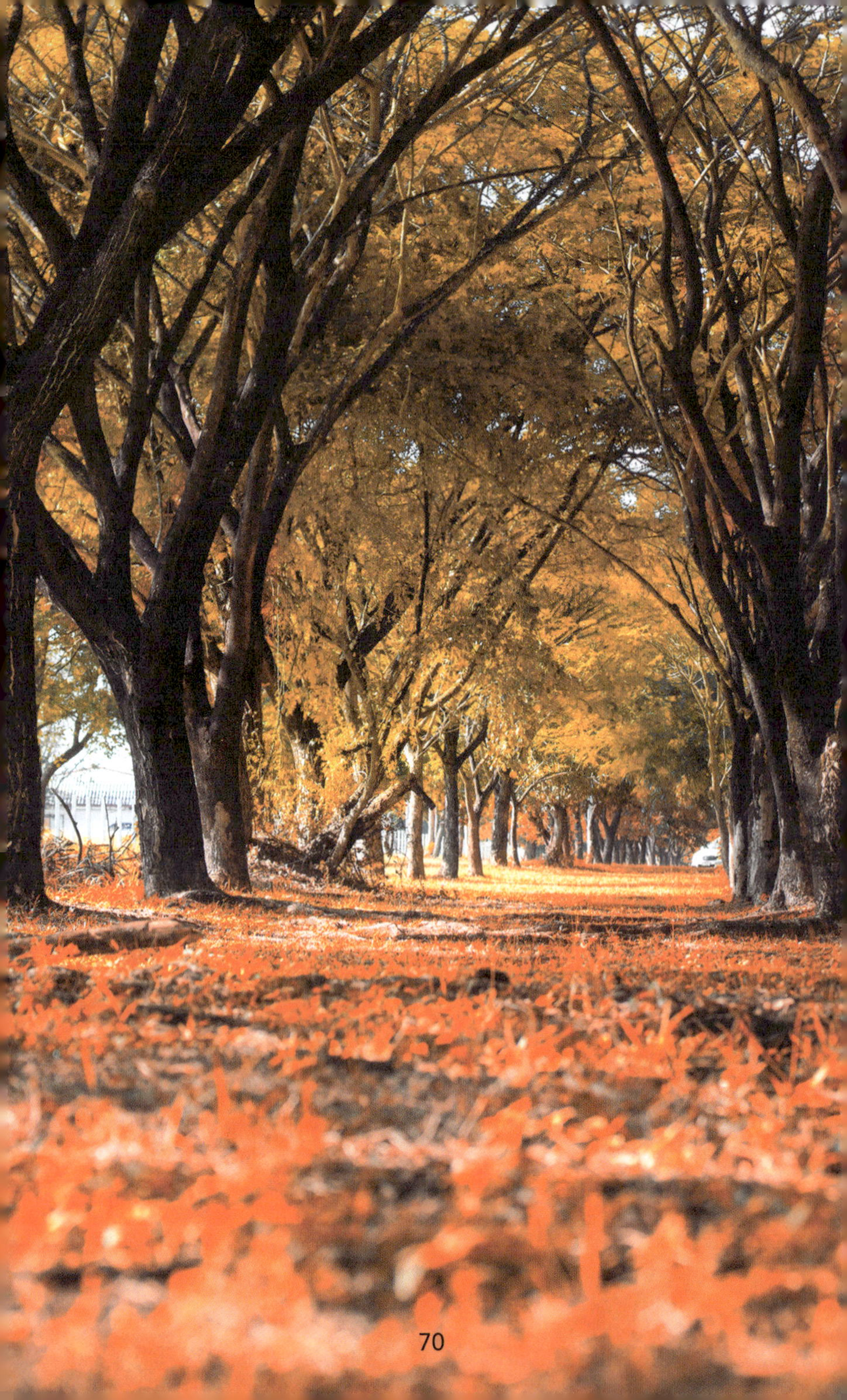

Autumn Walk

Today, come! Walk on high
Close to God beneath an Autumn sky.
A jay cries and a feather of that sky's own hue
Drifts down to mix its cobalt blue
With aspen gold and scrub oak red
Upon brown grass and green moss bed.
Now and then, a lone squirrel chatters.
All done with busy Summer matters.
The singing birds have flown…
Jay, chickadee and junco stay alone.
Here the flame of Fall leaps high,
There only bronzing embers lie
And spread their pearly smoke
Above the pine and oak.
Let my song rise with the misty haze
To thank God for the glory of Fall days.

Minnie Boyd Popish

*Your love is before
my eyes; I walk guided by
Your faithfulness.
Psalm 26:3*

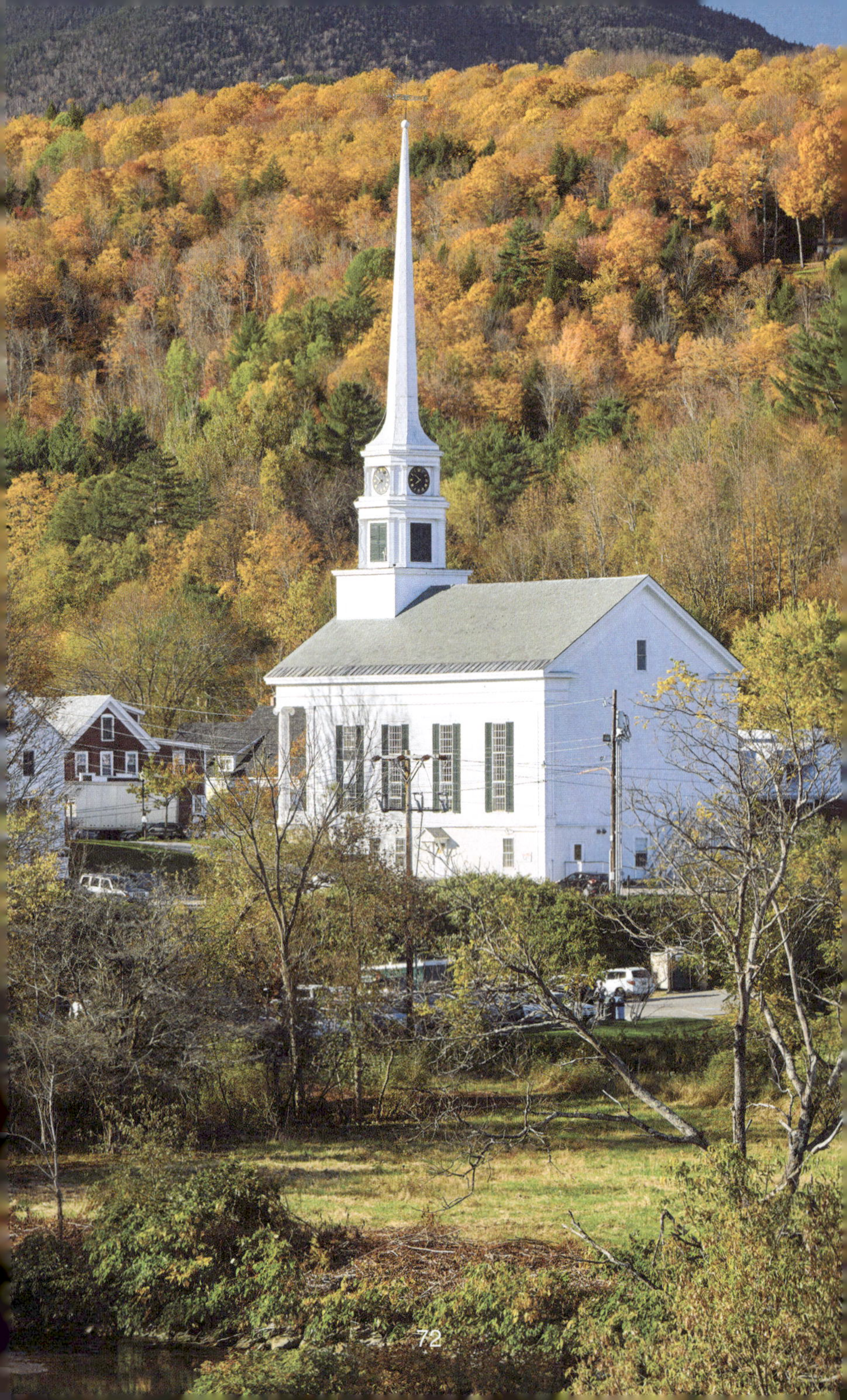

Let Us Welcome Fall

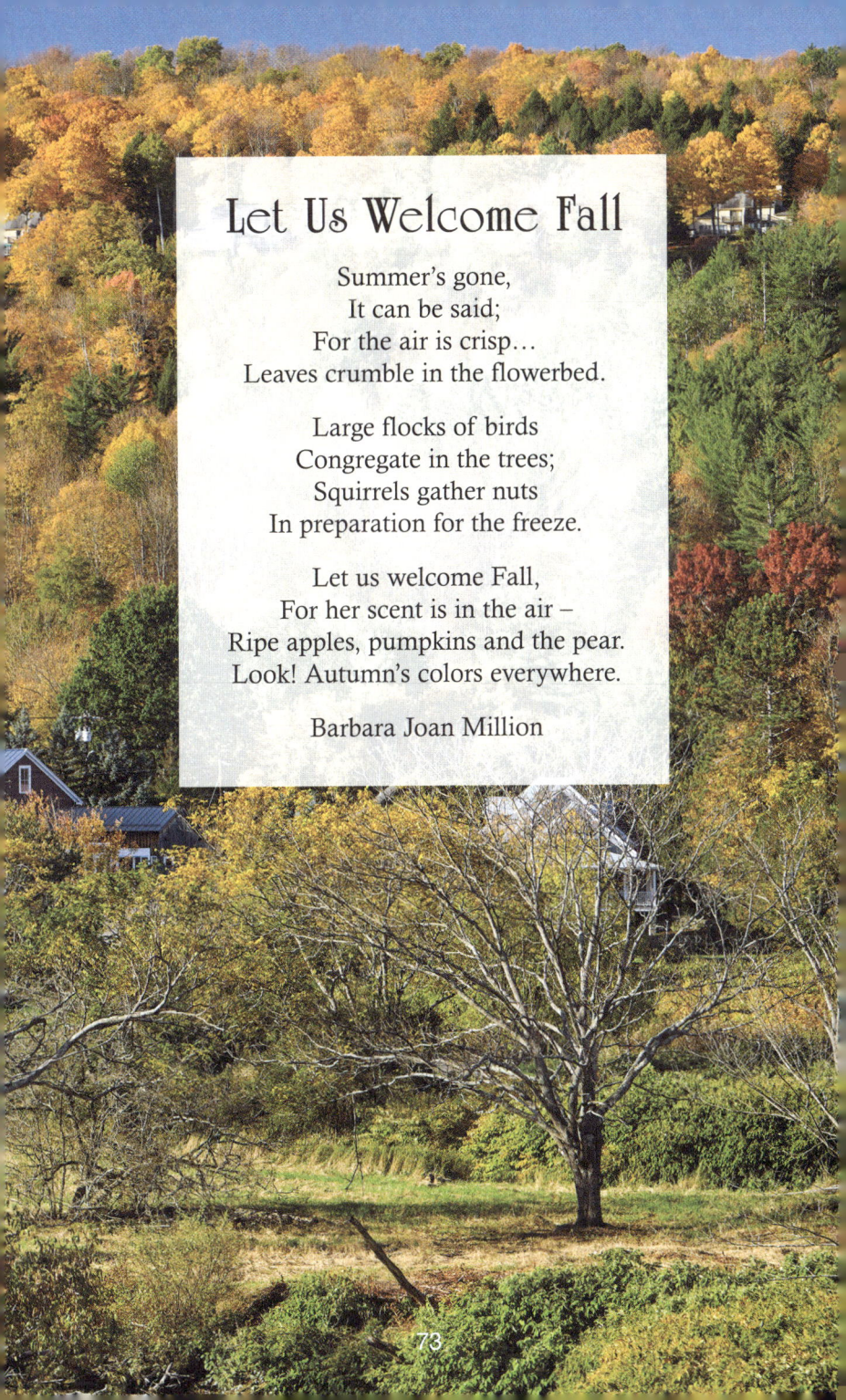

Summer's gone,
It can be said;
For the air is crisp…
Leaves crumble in the flowerbed.

Large flocks of birds
Congregate in the trees;
Squirrels gather nuts
In preparation for the freeze.

Let us welcome Fall,
For her scent is in the air –
Ripe apples, pumpkins and the pear.
Look! Autumn's colors everywhere.

Barbara Joan Million

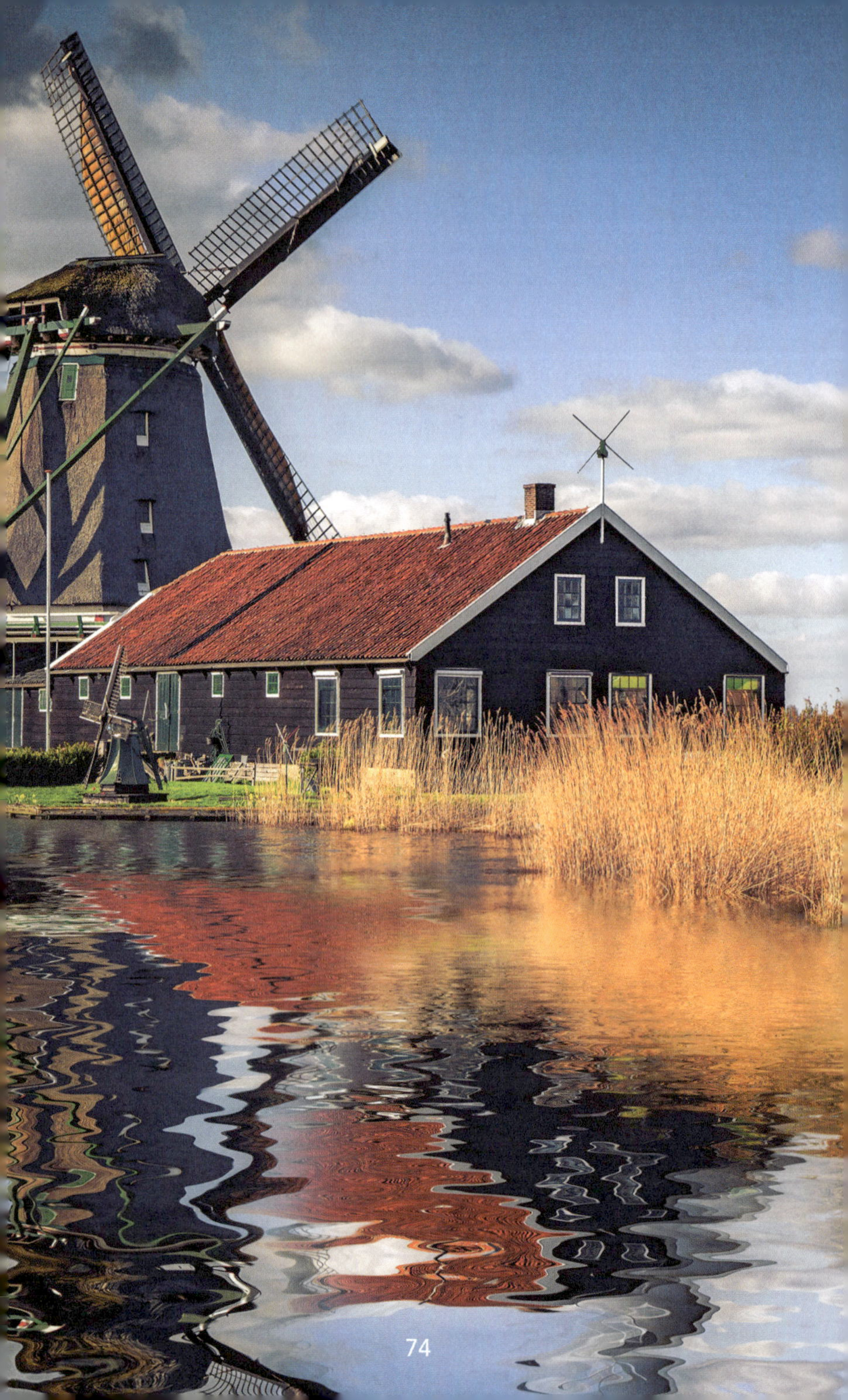

Autumn's Footsteps

I hear the sounds of Autumn,
They're blowing in the wind;
The balmy days of Summer
Are slowly growing dim.

The days are getting shorter,
The nights grow longer now;
The summertime's preparing
To take its final bow.

The birdsong has diminished,
And bird families are enroute
To sunny, sunny southland
Where flowers now flaunt their blooms.

The squirrels are gathering acorns
And tucking them in sod;
Throughout the flower garden
Are ripened milkweed pods.

I hear the Autumn footsteps,
They're coming around the bend;
In God's own time the Autumn
Will follow Summer's end.

Loise Pinkerton Fritz

Autumn Pie

Have a cup of sunshine
And a sip of Autumn breeze.
Put your feet up on the chair
And look up at the trees.
Stretch a bit – relax, unwind,
And sigh a great big sigh.
Look about at Nature's table,
Have some Autumn pie.
Love is in the air for birds on branches,
Leaves are raining down.
Step upon them, hear them crunching –
Autumn's come to town.

Reach down low and pick them up
And throw them to the sky.
Feel them falling, falling –
It's another slice of pie.
There's still more, some slices waiting,
And they're all for free.
Scent and sound and senseless beauty,
There... for you and me.

Dolores Dahl

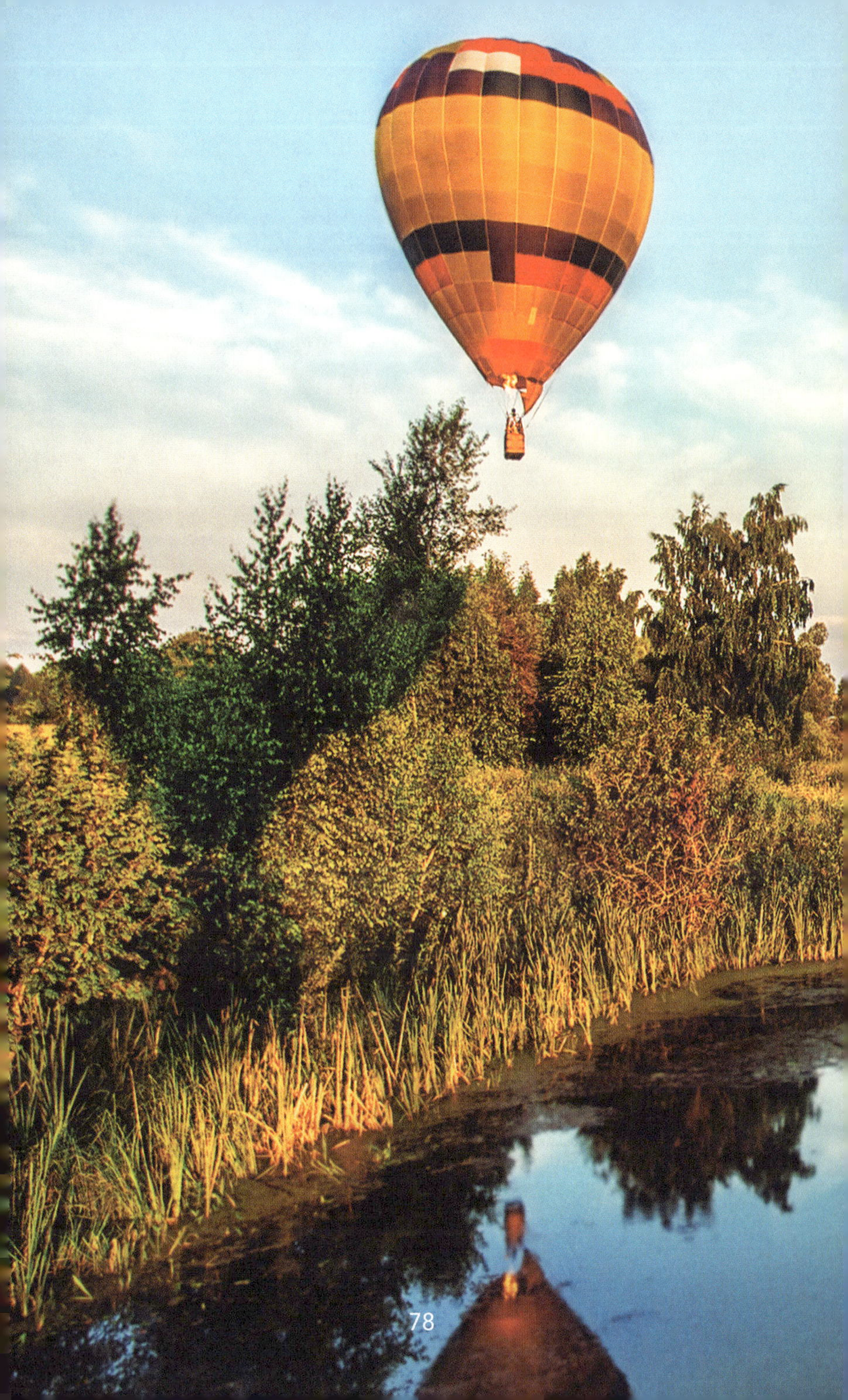

Golden Peace

Lord – fill me with Your golden peace,
Wildflowers and thistle down fleece.
Your bright blue skies and trees so red
And paths where purple asters spread.

To Your golden altar, I will go;
Through silken, soft leaves, I will toe.
Where scarlet maples lace the sky
And mountains reach above my eye.

Lord – fill me with the blithesome air,
The golds and reds just everywhere.
And I will follow the nomad bee
Where flowers bloom in ecstasy.

I will embrace the golden peace
And watch the flight of many geese.
This Autumn day, so bright and fair,
When trees hold gold within their hair.

Patricia Sarazen

*The Lord look upon you
kindly and give you peace!
Numbers 6:26*

Awesome Wonder

I sit in awesome wonder
Mesmerized by the beauty of Fall,
The last explosion of color
Before Winter makes its call.

The hills are lined with pillars of gold
With red jewels scattered by their side,
And orange and greens are entwined
Where wild grapevines appear to be tied.

I can't get enough of the beauty
Even though I truly try;
It's so hard to let go of the colors
Knowing soon it shall all die.

Row after row of red sumac
Glistens by the sassafras fair;
All add to the beauty of Autumn
Before north winds shake them bare.

Autumn is surely the crown jewel
Of every season on earth,
So I must remember the elegance
Until Spring brings us new birth.

We must hold on to good memories
And let them linger long in our mind;
God presented us with Autumn,
His ultimate gift to mankind.

Shirley Hile Powell

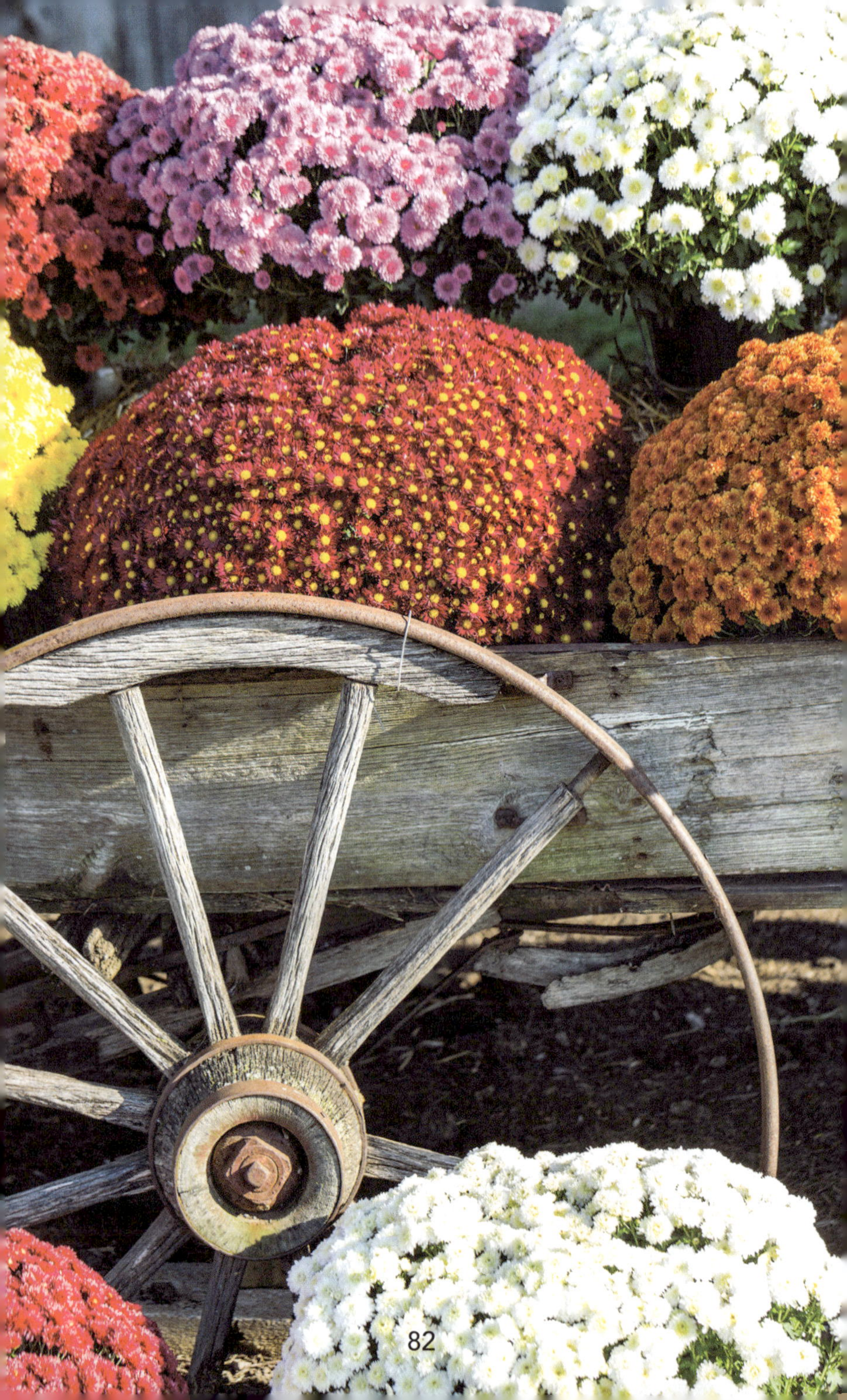

Planting

Plant peace throughout your garden,
For without it problems grow,
And choke out all the blessings
That otherwise would flow.
Let grace o'ertake the worries,
And sow calm among that grief;
Put in some roots of kindness…
Sweet love nurtures relief.
The blossoms of forgiveness
Extinguish anger sown
By those who were never gardeners
Or on their knees had grown
To know the Master Gardener…
In His garden blooms tall joy.
Choose well your garden plantings
And therein your heart employ.

Ruthmarie Brooks Silver

*Turn again, Lord of hosts; look
down from Heaven and see;
Attend to this vine, the shoot
Your right hand has planted.
Psalm 80:15-16*

Autumn Sunrise

There's a rare and awesome beauty
About a sunrise in the Fall
As the sun emerges in the east –
A huge and glowing ball
Of fiery red and orange
Against a dull and hazy sky,
It sprays a brilliant rose-effect
That's pleasing to the eye.
As it continues upward from behind
The silhouetted mountains,
It pierces mist and spews forth light,
Just as the flowing fountains.

The hillsides and ridges stand tall –
Casting their shadows across the way
On this perfect Autumn morning…
Marking the beginning of a new day.
Overhead the clouds are brilliant
As they float o'er mountain peaks.
They display a melon lining;
Some are fluffy, some mere streaks.
As you look upon this sunrise
With its beauty so sublime,
Oh, that you could forever capture it
And stop the hands of time.
But, alas, too soon its beauty fades –
The color's nearly gone.
And each must go about his work
As time continues on.
I know my God is very pleased
From Heaven's point of view
To look upon a sunrise
With its glorious ray of hue.
So one day when we expect it least,
And need a little lift,
He'll provide another radiant sunrise –
A majestic, loving gift.

Geraldine Borger

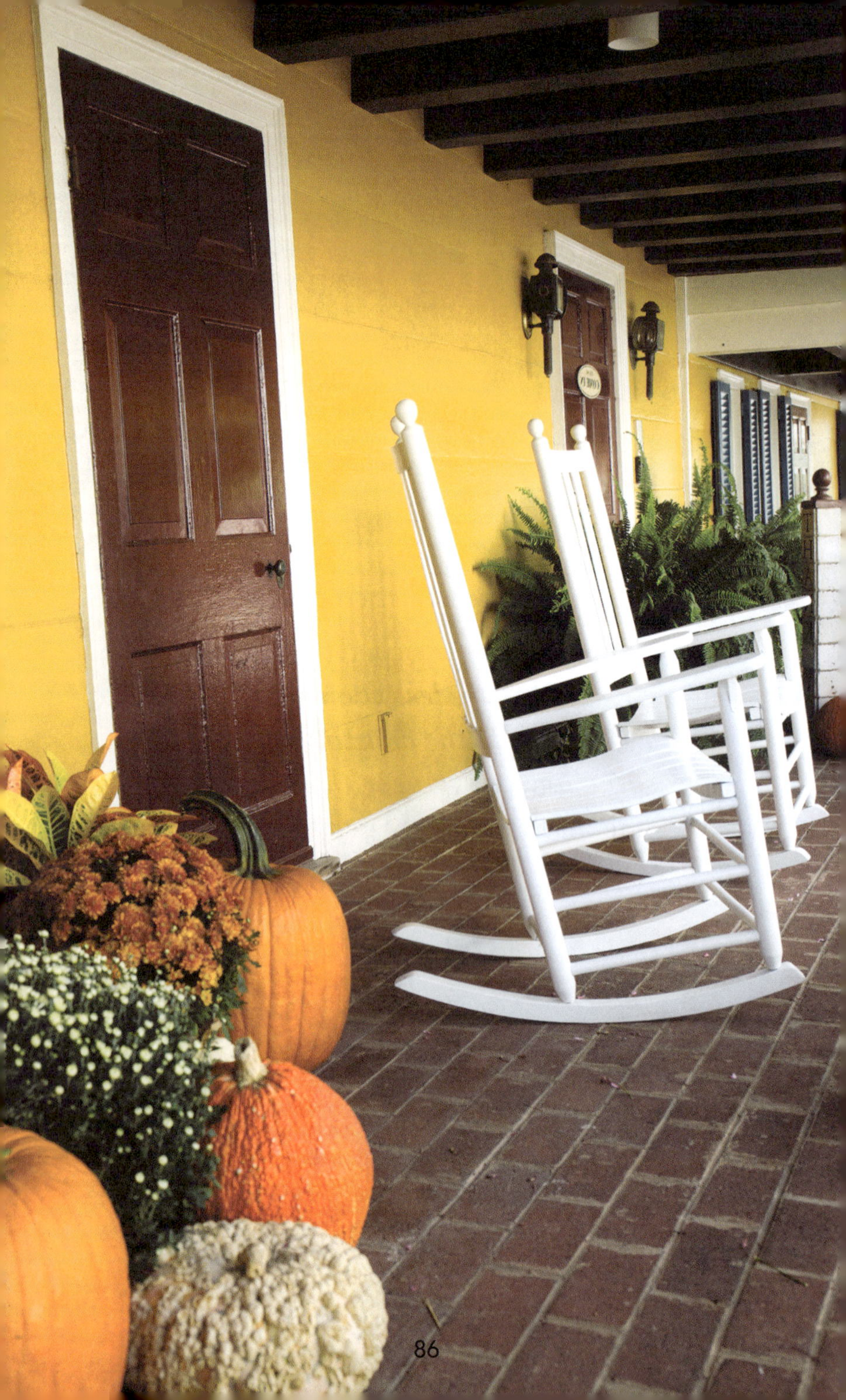

Dear Lord...

*Thank You for the harvest
and the wonderful crops that grow.
Please let there be plentiful harvest
so there is enough food for everyone.
Help us to be generous
and to share what we have with those
who have less than us.
Let us treat the amazing world
You have given us with respect
and help us to make good choices.*

Amen

Life in Autumn

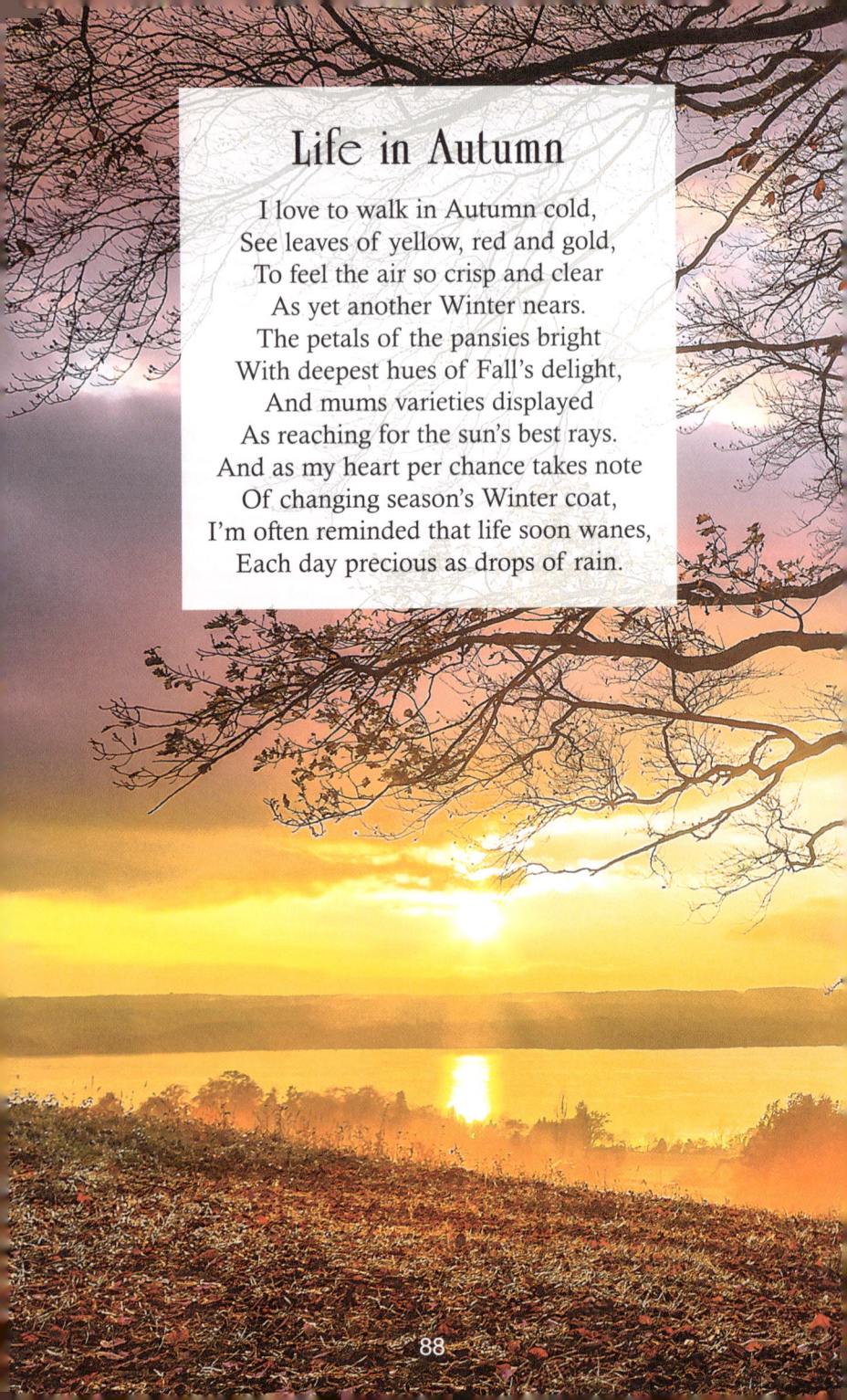

I love to walk in Autumn cold,
See leaves of yellow, red and gold,
To feel the air so crisp and clear
As yet another Winter nears.
The petals of the pansies bright
With deepest hues of Fall's delight,
And mums varieties displayed
As reaching for the sun's best rays.
And as my heart per chance takes note
Of changing season's Winter coat,
I'm often reminded that life soon wanes,
Each day precious as drops of rain.

The time we're given by God above
Should be spent in peace and love,
Knowing seasons are but a sign
Of greater things in His own time.
For when the portals open wide
And we see Jesus on the other side,
Our time spent here will seem but small –
At struggle's end we'll have won all.

Lynda Bryan Davis

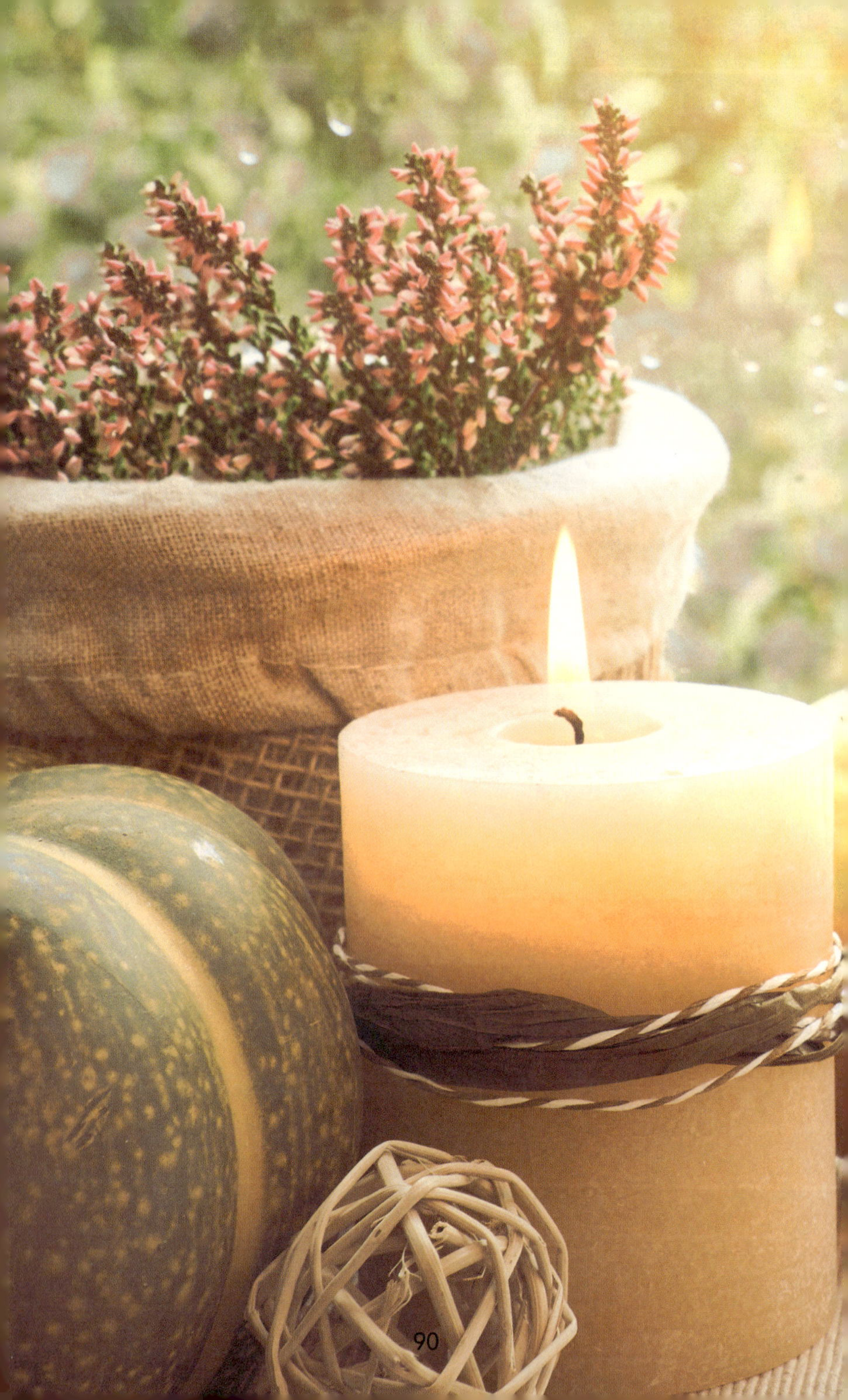

Picturesque Beauty

Fall fast approaching,
Colorful scenes,
Leaving the Summer
Only in dreams.

Flowers close their blossoms,
Fall fast asleep,
Tuck away bright colors,
All in God's keep.

Frost soon arriving,
Paints everything;
Crisp is the Autumn
Waiting in wing.

Snowflakes of splendor
Softly in sound,
Picturesque beauty,
Blanket the ground.

Katherine Smith Matheney

Autumn

How caring is our wondrous God
Who sends the autumntime,
With beauty that uplifts the heart
And makes each day sublime.

The dazzling hills of red and gold
Proclaim His majesty;
A scene that only God could paint,
So splendrous to see.

The tawny fields of ripened grain,
Rich bounty from His hand;
Enough to share with those in need
Whatever be their land.

A bluish haze on distant hills,
Flower beds in colors bright;
Fat pumpkins heaped along the wall
Await a child's delight.

The sunset's flame of burnished gold
That marks the close of day;
A view that's so breathtaking,
I brush a tear away.

I'm thankful for each season
Endowed with beauty rare;
Still, it's in the Autumn of the year
That I see God everywhere.

Kay Hoffman

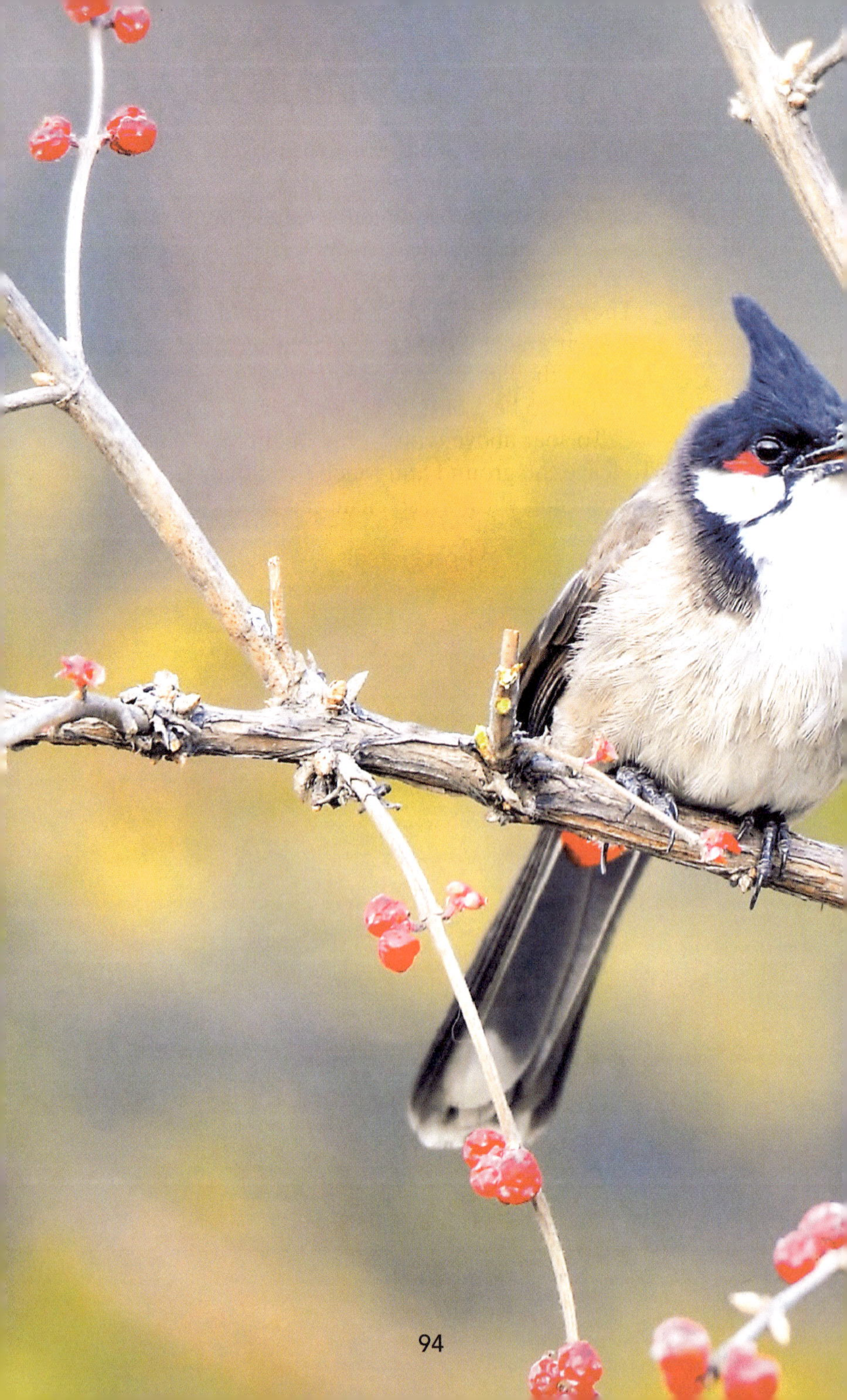

Birds Take Flight

In the meadow green and fair,
Birds take flight into the air.
Their wings spread wide, they soar so high
In the boundless, open sky.
With feathers bright and colors bold,
They paint the sky with stories untold.
Their graceful dance, a sight to see,
As they glide and roam so free.
Oh, to be a bird and take flight,
To soar above with all my might.
To leave the ground and touch the clouds,
And sing with joy, so clear and loud.

AI-generated

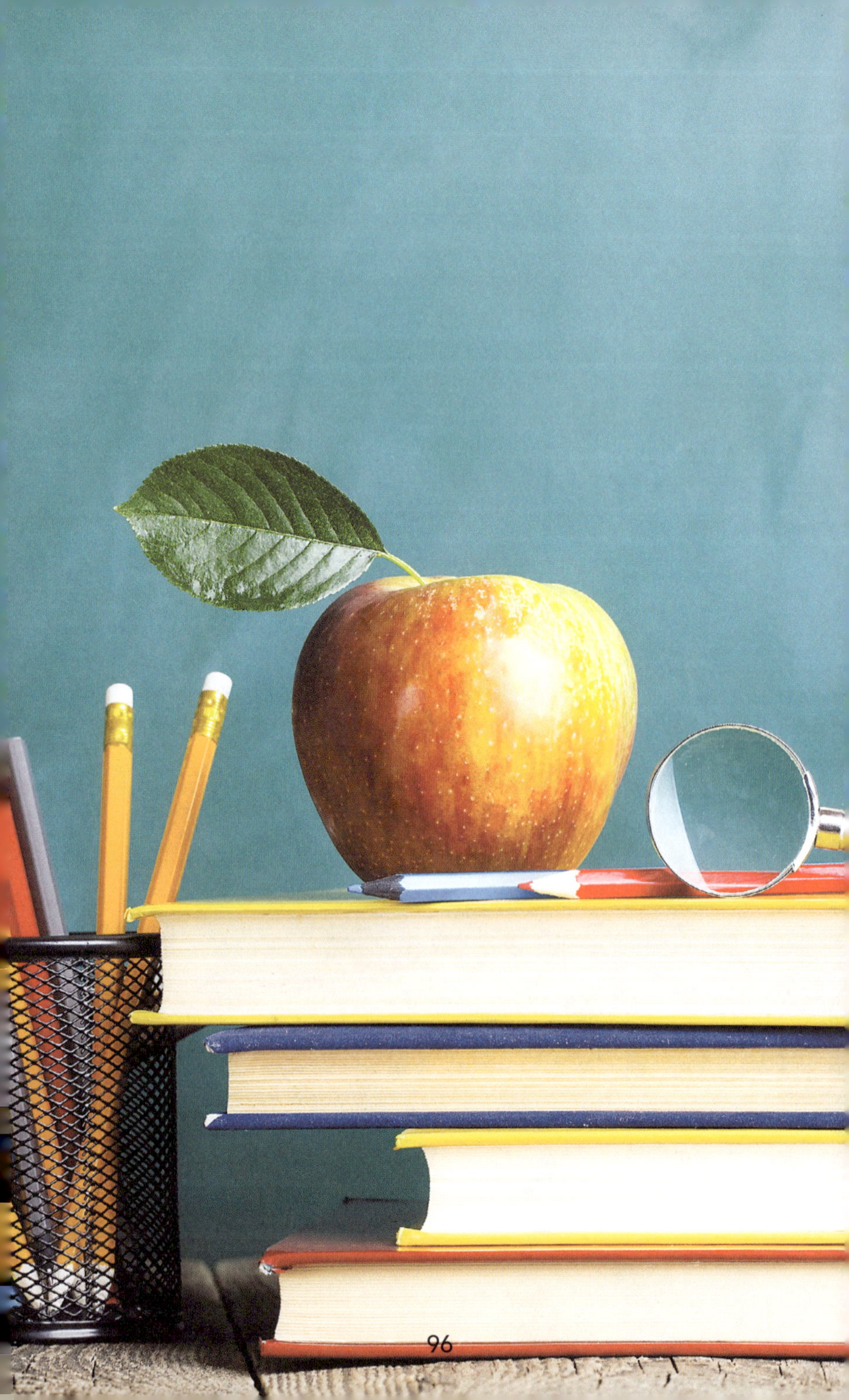

September's Voice

September's voice seems sad at times:
It calls the students back to class;
Reminds the flowers they will fade,
And brown shall turn the withered grass!

Mournful its message we must heed:
Our "Summer days" too quickly pass,
And that bright mirror of our youth
Shall dim like broken shards of glass!

And yet, it joyfully forecasts
The golden haze of Autumn days,
When purple hills are kissed by frost
'Til Winter brings the holidays!

Then surely grass will go to seed,
Our fallow time will also pass;
September's voice grows glad indeed,
And speaks of Spring to come at last.

Where flowers bloom that do not fade,
And Someone welcomes to His class
Students whose Summers never end
Nor spirits dim like shattered glass!

John C. Bonser

Winter Morning

'Tis early morn and the day is born
With Winter air crisp and clear.
There is no sound to hear around:
Silence is far and near.
No sign can be found on the snowy ground
Of man or bird or beast.
All the world's asleep 'neath a blanket so deep;
A blanket of heavenly peace.
My thoughts gently stray to a land far away
Where hosts of angels sing;
Dressed in white and shining so bright
With the glory of Jesus their King.

There are no cares or sorrows there,
Never a mournful tone.
There is no night, and the warmth and the light
Come from the One on the throne.
The soul finds serenity with the legacy
Of the human family;
United as one with God's only Son
In peace eternally.
The new-fallen snow helps me to know
The peace God's spirit gives;
His glory is found in this snow on the ground
And in everything that lives.

Steven Michael Schumacher

Bringing Out
the Best of Winter

To bring out the best of Winter,
We need to view it optimistically
By enjoying the moments and hours
With a youthful spirit, enthusiastic and carefree!
Watching the snowflakes tumble and twirl,
Pirouetting high up in the sky;
Oh look for the wonder in Winter
And transform that sad frown and weary sigh.
Stomp about in those heavy, leather boots
In search of a raccoon, buck or doe,
Then chuckle at a furry, brown groundhog
As he comes out to peek at the pristine snow!

Mostly all the leaves have fallen,
And flocks of geese instinctively headed south;
Yet, God designed so much sparkle to admire
That it seems a snow globe of Winter surrounds.
Bringing out the best in wintertime
May not be an easy task,
But for a brief time just grin and bear it
And thank God, Winter doesn't forever last.

Linda C. Grazulis

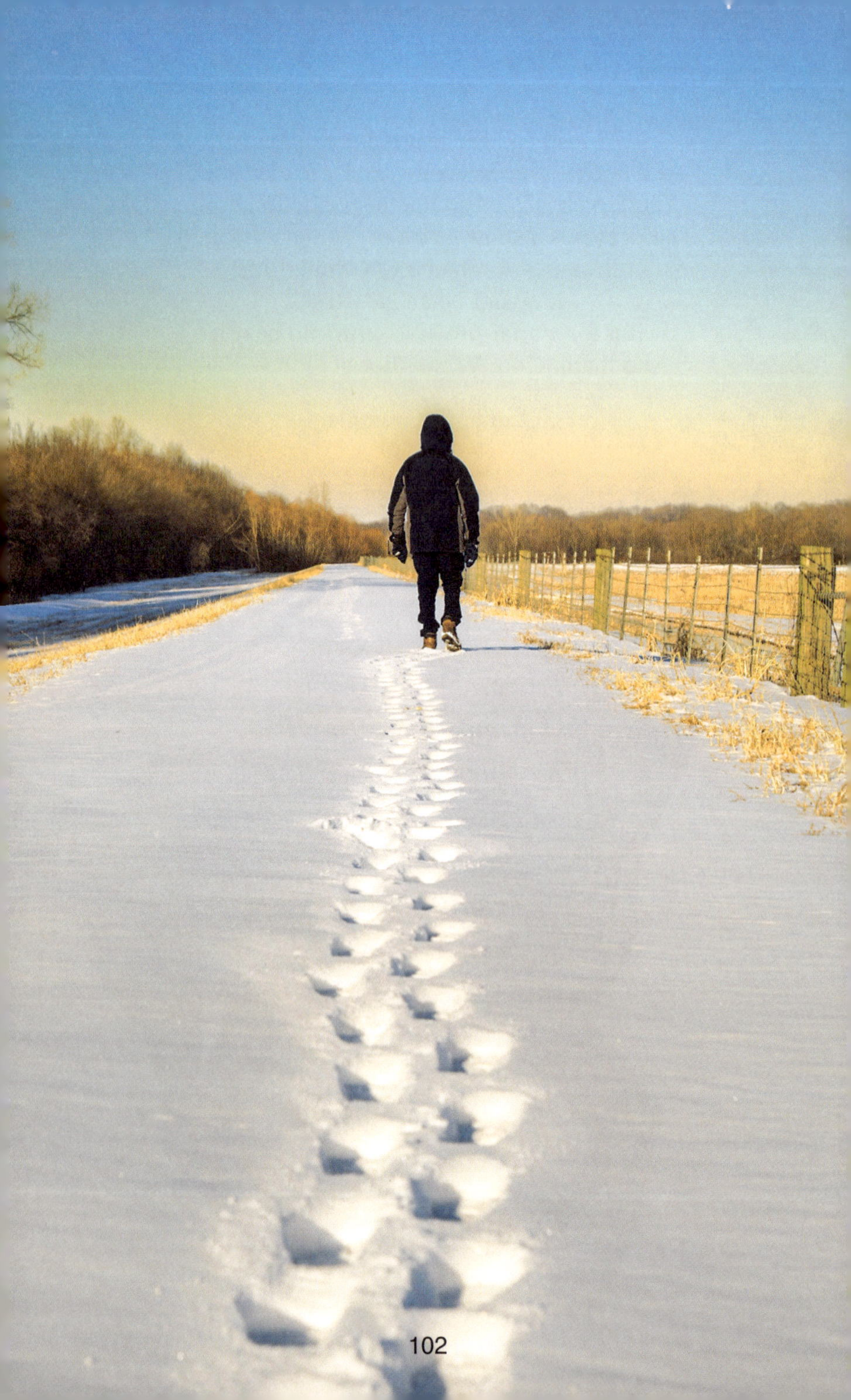

Lord God

*When I wake in the morning,
may the rising sun
and the new day
remind me to always
begin my day with You.
To praise You
and thank You for Your
faithfulness to me.
To lean on You when
I need strength and support.
To request Your mercy
when I need a fresh start.
To know that You will be
my bright light when
my day looks dark.*

Amen

Winter Wonder

A small, beautiful snowflake,
Created by earth's gentlest Man…
Each crystal glows like diamonds –
Gently touched by a child's hand.
This child is God's little angel,
So awed by the wonder of snow…
Our Savior looks down, smiling –
This child, with his face aglow.
Beautiful etching on each window,
As only our Lord can create…
Winter's splendor at its very best –
Each design perfectly ornate.
The child gently traces the artwork,
With his little finger in play…
This pure happiness of discovery –
On his very first Winter day!

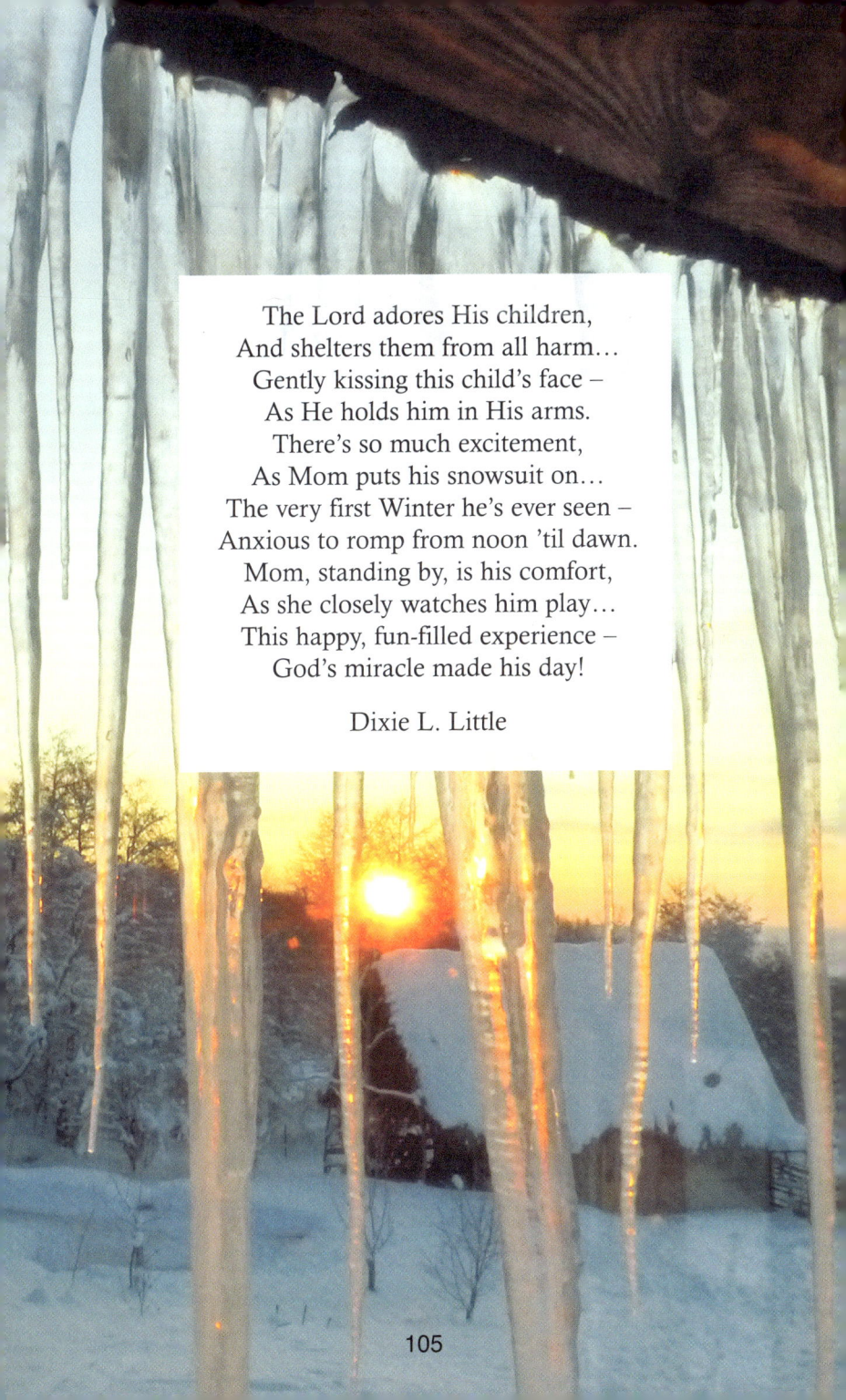

The Lord adores His children,
And shelters them from all harm…
Gently kissing this child's face –
As He holds him in His arms.
There's so much excitement,
As Mom puts his snowsuit on…
The very first Winter he's ever seen –
Anxious to romp from noon 'til dawn.
Mom, standing by, is his comfort,
As she closely watches him play…
This happy, fun-filled experience –
God's miracle made his day!

Dixie L. Little

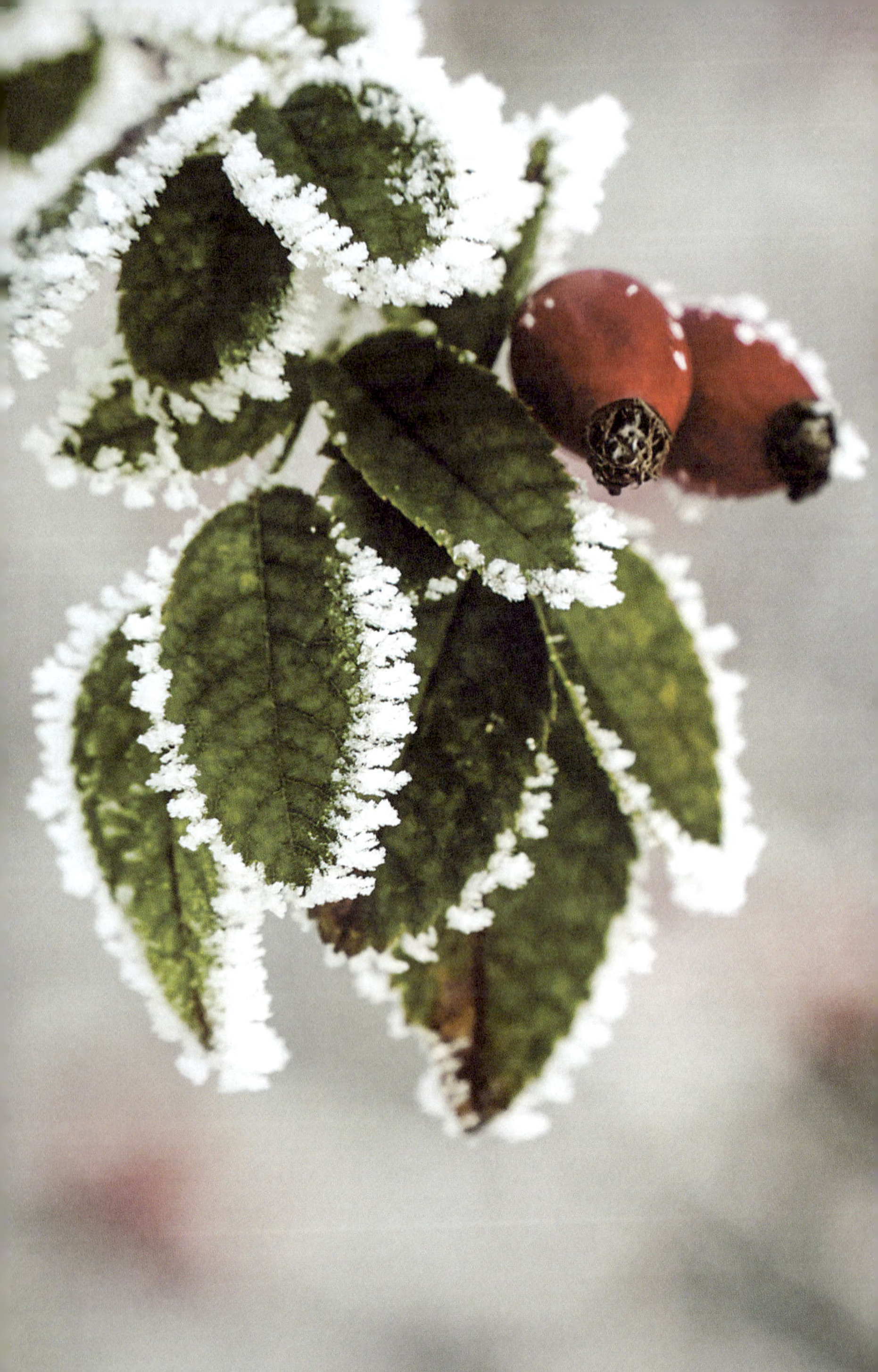

A Crystal World

We're living in a crystal world…
It's wonderful to be
Where shining crystal bushes bow
Beneath a glass-encrusted tree;
Where each sparkling blade of grass
Stands erect and tall
And scintillating rotund weeds
Are most brilliant of all.

We travel on a crystal road
With fear and trepidation –
Lest we slip from the narrow way
Into utter deprivation!
Timidly we now proceed
With measured steps and slow;
This world is a tranquil sea
With treacherous undertow.

R.J. Tabberer

*I have heard that the spirit
of God is in you, that you
possess brilliant knowledge
and extraordinary wisdom.
Daniel 5:14*

Winter Sunrise

At first, all dark and dreary,
So cold this frosty air;
There's just a glint of light now,
But still too cold to care!
Then, along the southern sky,
A glimpse of faintest blue;
While high above, the dark gray clouds
Take on a pinkish hue.
Indeed the sun is rising
As it starts today's big show;
Those dark clouds farther out now
Take on a reddish glow.
And soon the sky's afire
As we view this fleeting scene;
The clouds now red to gray,
And all hues in between.

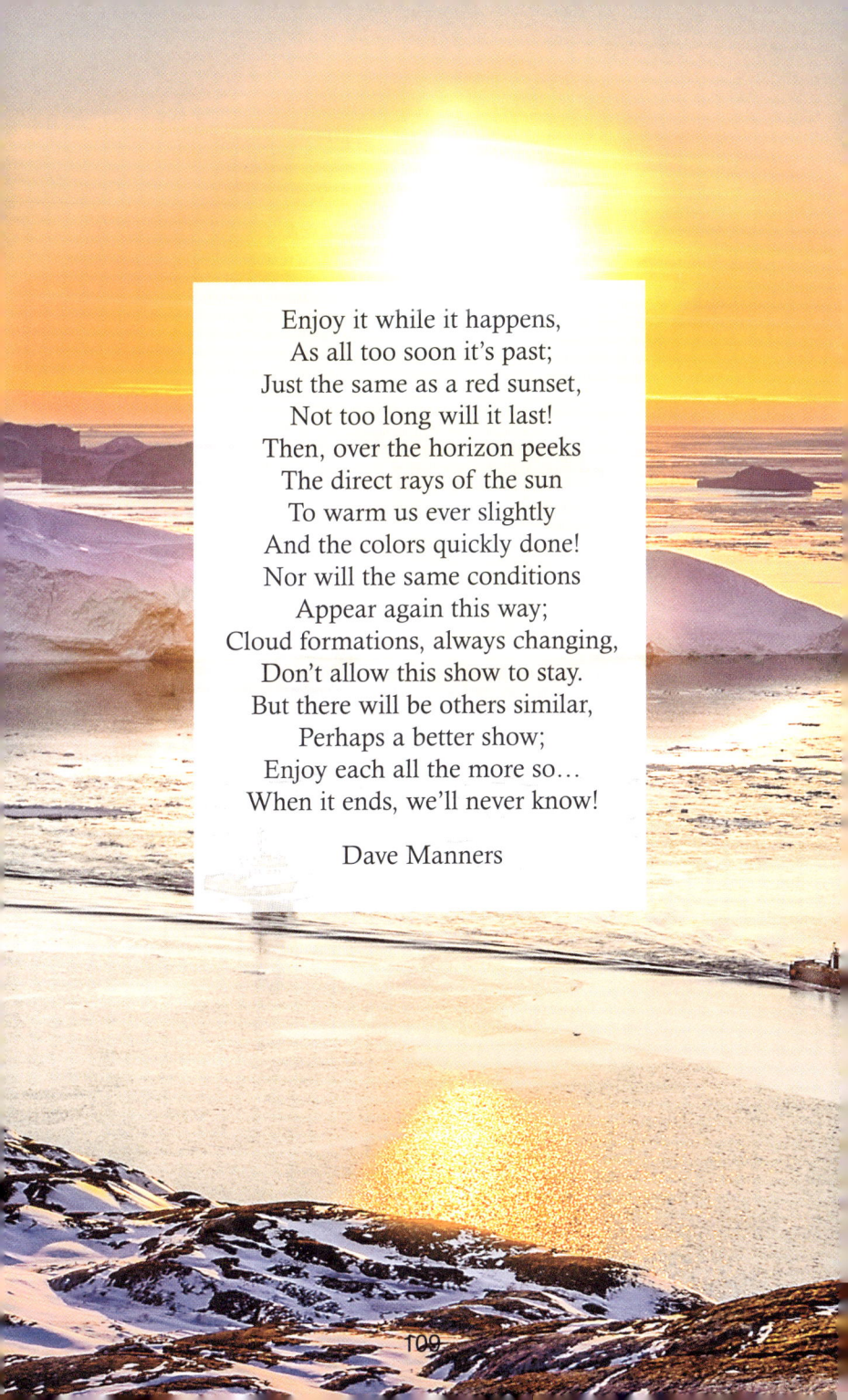

Enjoy it while it happens,
As all too soon it's past;
Just the same as a red sunset,
Not too long will it last!
Then, over the horizon peeks
The direct rays of the sun
To warm us ever slightly
And the colors quickly done!
Nor will the same conditions
Appear again this way;
Cloud formations, always changing,
Don't allow this show to stay.
But there will be others similar,
Perhaps a better show;
Enjoy each all the more so…
When it ends, we'll never know!

Dave Manners

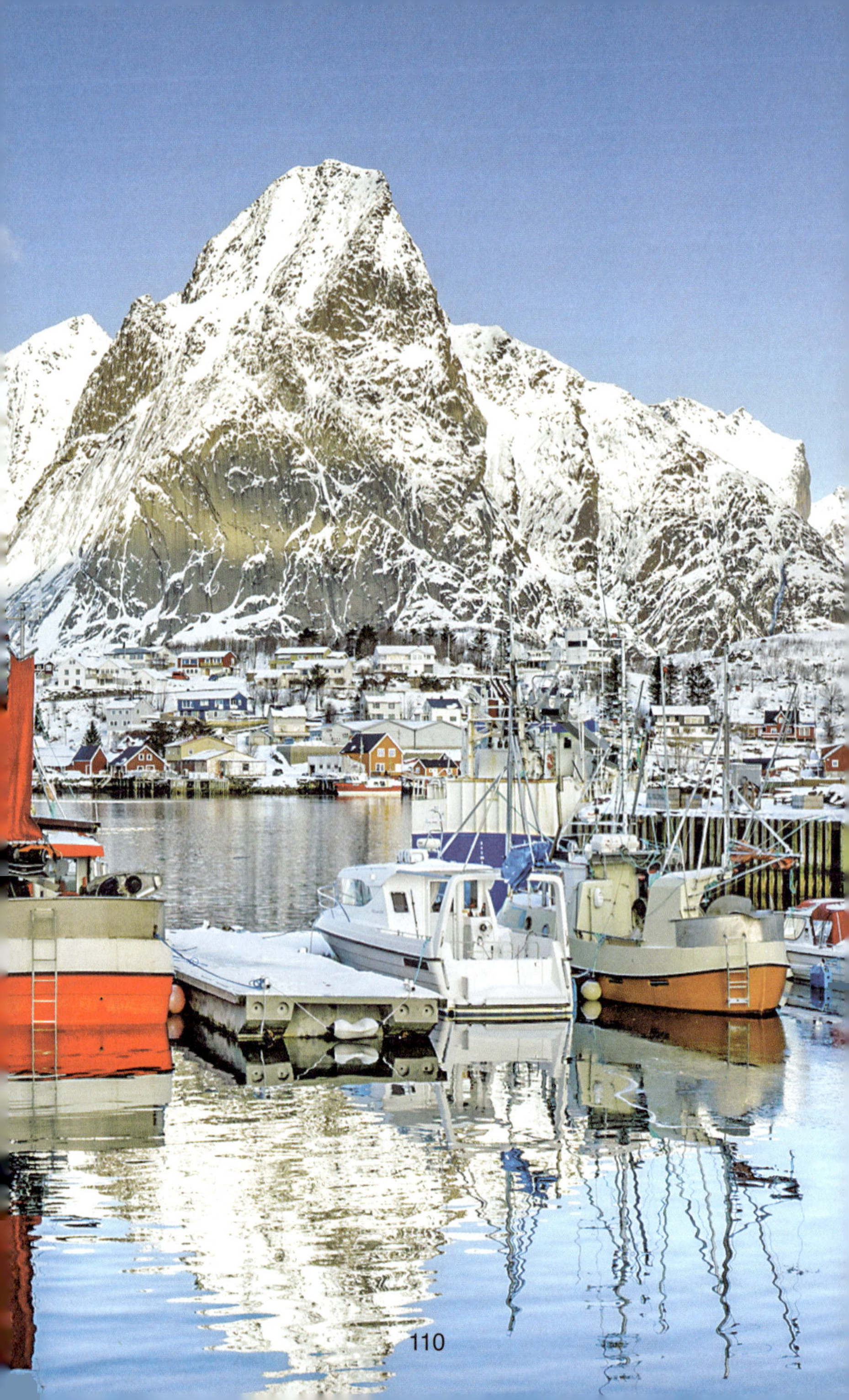

Snowflakes

The gently blowing wind
Embraces falling snowflakes,
Escorting them to earth,
And not a sound it makes.

Lacy snowflakes cluster
On limbs of naked trees,
Clothing them in dazzling white,
Aided by the gentle breeze.

The snowflakes softly kiss
The tips of every nose,
Touching blinking eyelashes
As down to earth they go.

Now maybe a snowflake
Is an angel in disguise,
And only by the children
Are they recognized.

An angel snowflake
Has no need of wings,
And the children say
The snowflake even sings.

Bernice Laux

But the wisdom from above is first of all pure, then peaceable, gentle, compliant, full of mercy and good fruits, without inconstancy or insincerity.
James 3:17

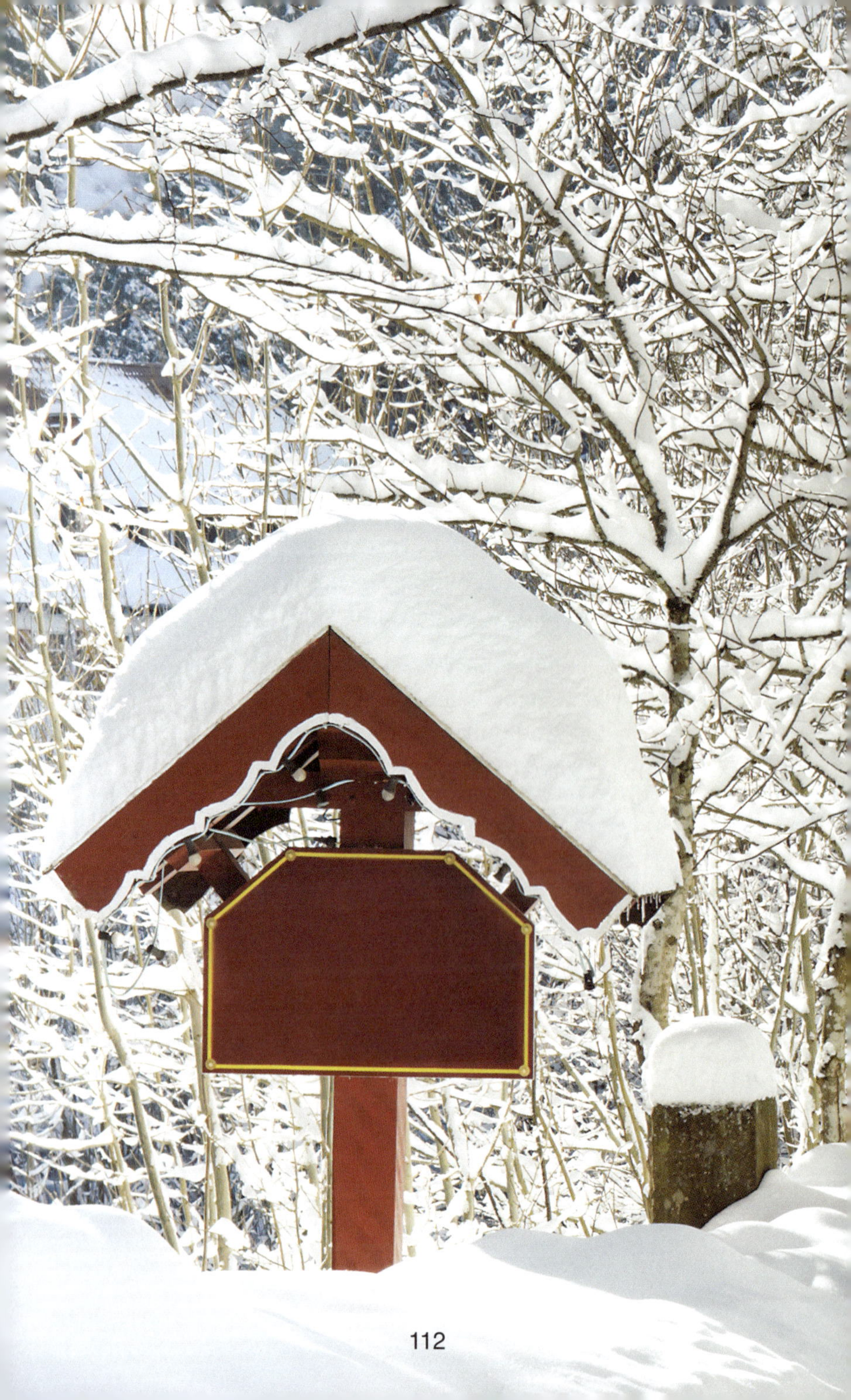

A Meadow Filled With Snow

Imagine a meadow filled with snow
On a late Winter day,
When every heart is filled with hope
That Spring's not far away.
The pewter skies will soon be blue
As days begin to warm;
And when there's clover in the meadow,
The bees again will swarm.
The snow will melt and fade away;
And the dogwoods shall bloom
And that meadow filled with snow
Shall lose its chilly gloom.
For everything there is a season
According to God's plan;
And our Winters of discontent
Are merely grains of sand…
Grains of sand in God's hourglass
As months and years unfold;
In time we'll see the dogwoods bloom
And Autumn's leaves of gold.
When nights are long and hearts are cold,
We sometimes fear the day;
But like that meadow filled with snow,
Spring's surely on the way!

Clay Harrison

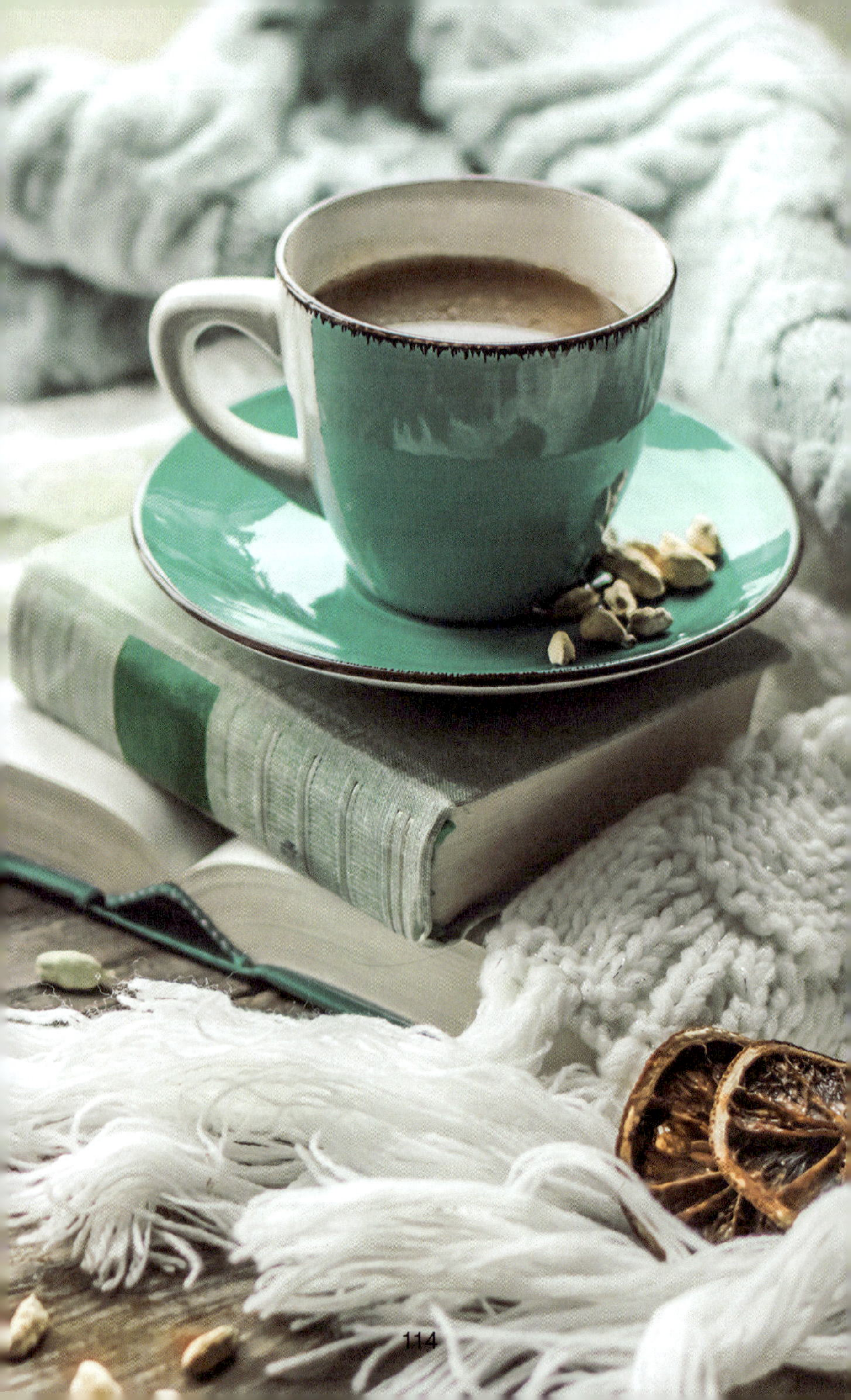

March Has Arrived

March has a way
Of reversing its role:
One day it's warm,
And another it's cold.

One day the Summer
Will seem to appear;
The next will be cold
Like the Winter is here.

Ofttimes the wind
Makes a furious sound;
Winter's dressed out in
A snowy white gown.

Soon, very soon,
There's a robin in quest,
Searching for somewhere
To build her nest.

Winter stopped by
And put on a display;
March has arrived
With a mixture array.

Snowflakes and sunbeams
And buds are all seen;
March paves the way
For the Summer's dress green.

Katherine Smith Matheney

Winter Is...

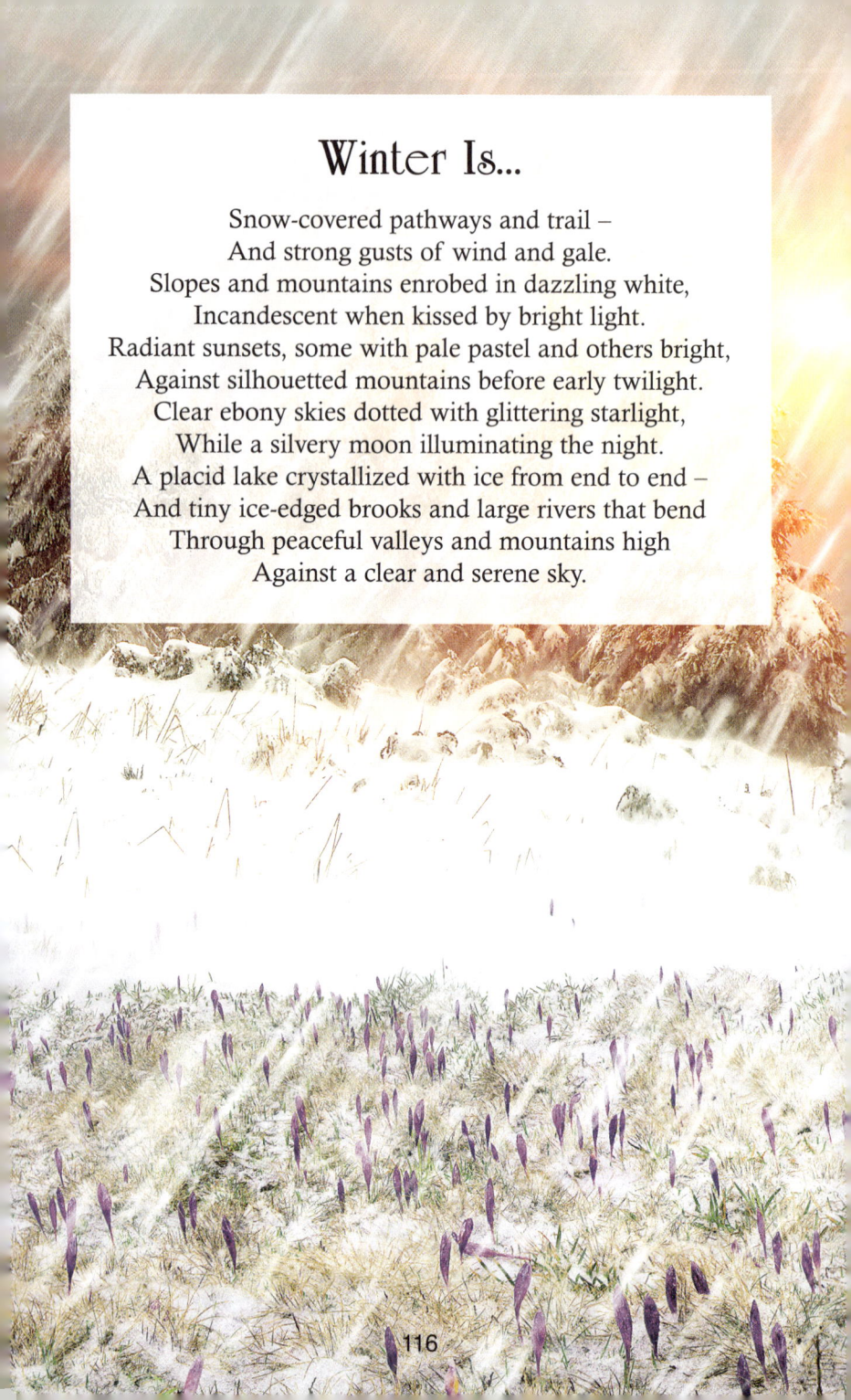

Snow-covered pathways and trail –
And strong gusts of wind and gale.
Slopes and mountains enrobed in dazzling white,
Incandescent when kissed by bright light.
Radiant sunsets, some with pale pastel and others bright,
Against silhouetted mountains before early twilight.
Clear ebony skies dotted with glittering starlight,
While a silvery moon illuminating the night.
A placid lake crystallized with ice from end to end –
And tiny ice-edged brooks and large rivers that bend
Through peaceful valleys and mountains high
Against a clear and serene sky.

Beautiful ducks and geese swimming gracefully –
Upon a partially frozen lake, until they flee
And take formation within the air,
In flight usually traveling in a pair.
The hemlock, the spruce and other evergreen,
With snowladen branches and ice in between,
Can be seen – While newly cut or decaying stumps
Sport mounds of snowcaps heaped in neat clumps.
Yes, Winter is sunsets and cold nights with star-studded sky,
Snow-laden trees, and ducks and geese flying by –
Ice-covered water and snow-covered sod
All are part of the Winter beauty created by God.

Geraldine Borger

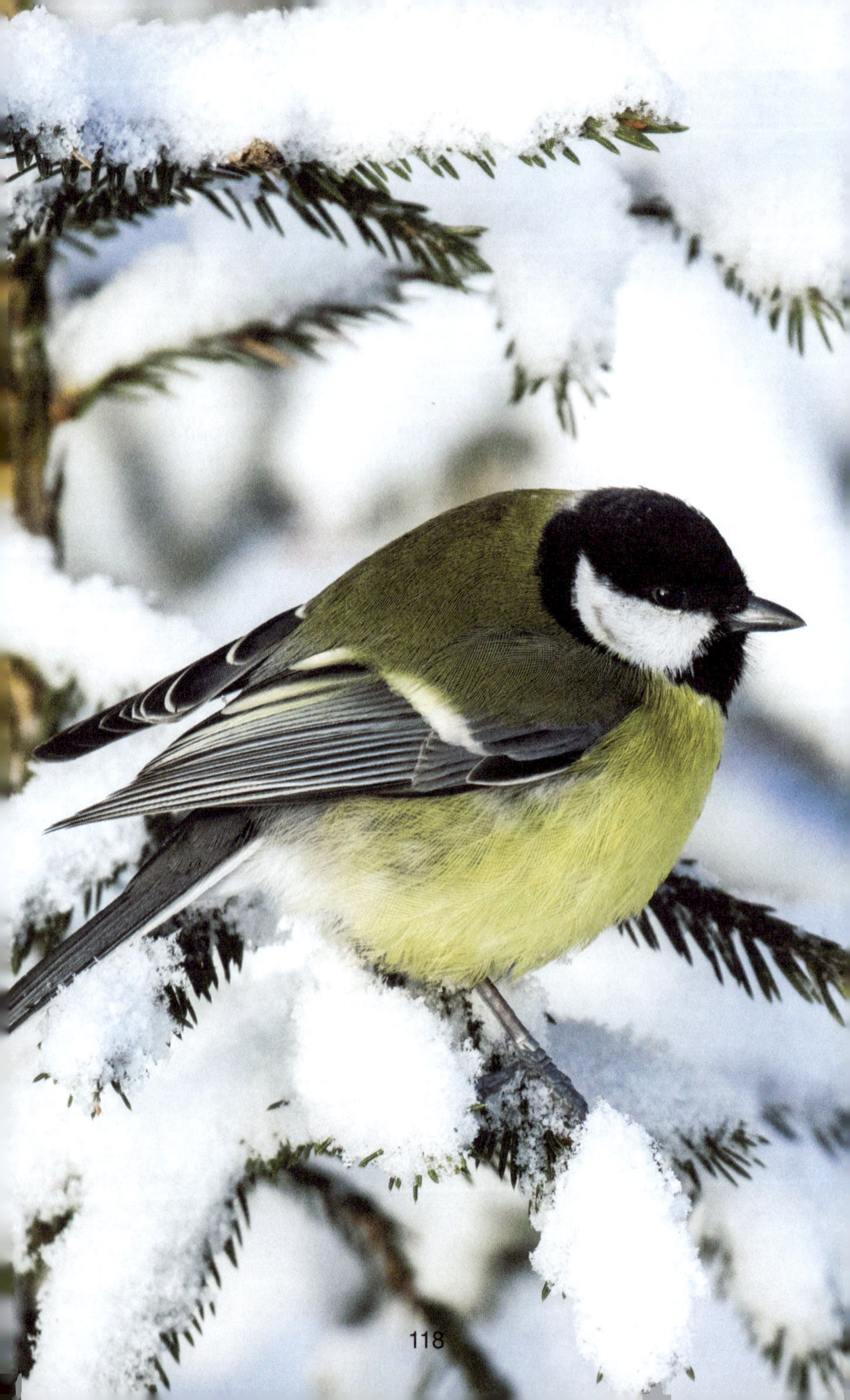

Prayer of St. Francis of Assisi

*Lord, make me an instrument of Your peace:
Where there is hatred, let me sow love;
where there is injury, pardon;
where there is doubt, faith;
where there is despair, hope;
where there is darkness, light;
where there is sadness, joy.*

*O Divine Master, grant that I may not
so much seek to be consoled as to console;
to be understood as to understand;
to be loved as to love.*

*For it is in giving that we receive;
it is in pardoning that we are pardoned;
and it is in dying that we are
born to eternal life.*

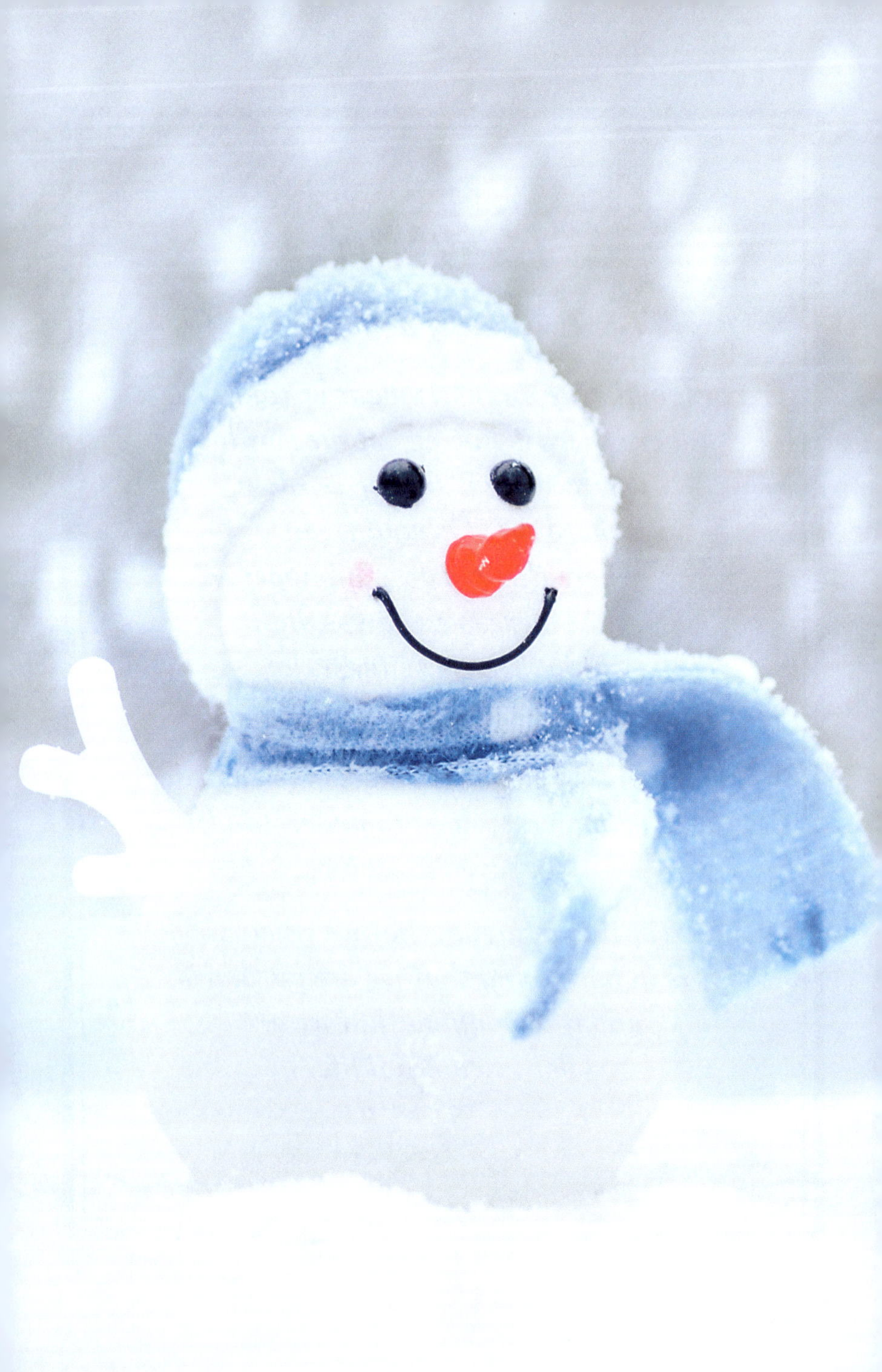

The Glory of Winter

Autumn's sheaves are frosted
Like statues of straw
In fields now deserted
'Til Spring's early thaw.
There is ice on the pond
With snow flurries today,
And Summer's blue skies
Are a memory away.
Soon there will be snowmen
In everyone's yard,
Each armed with a broomstick
For standing on guard.
We sit by the fireplace
With hearts all aglow,
Sipping steaming hot cider
While it's twenty below.
The glory of Winter
Sets the season apart,
For the beauty it brings
Is felt in the heart.

Clay Harrison

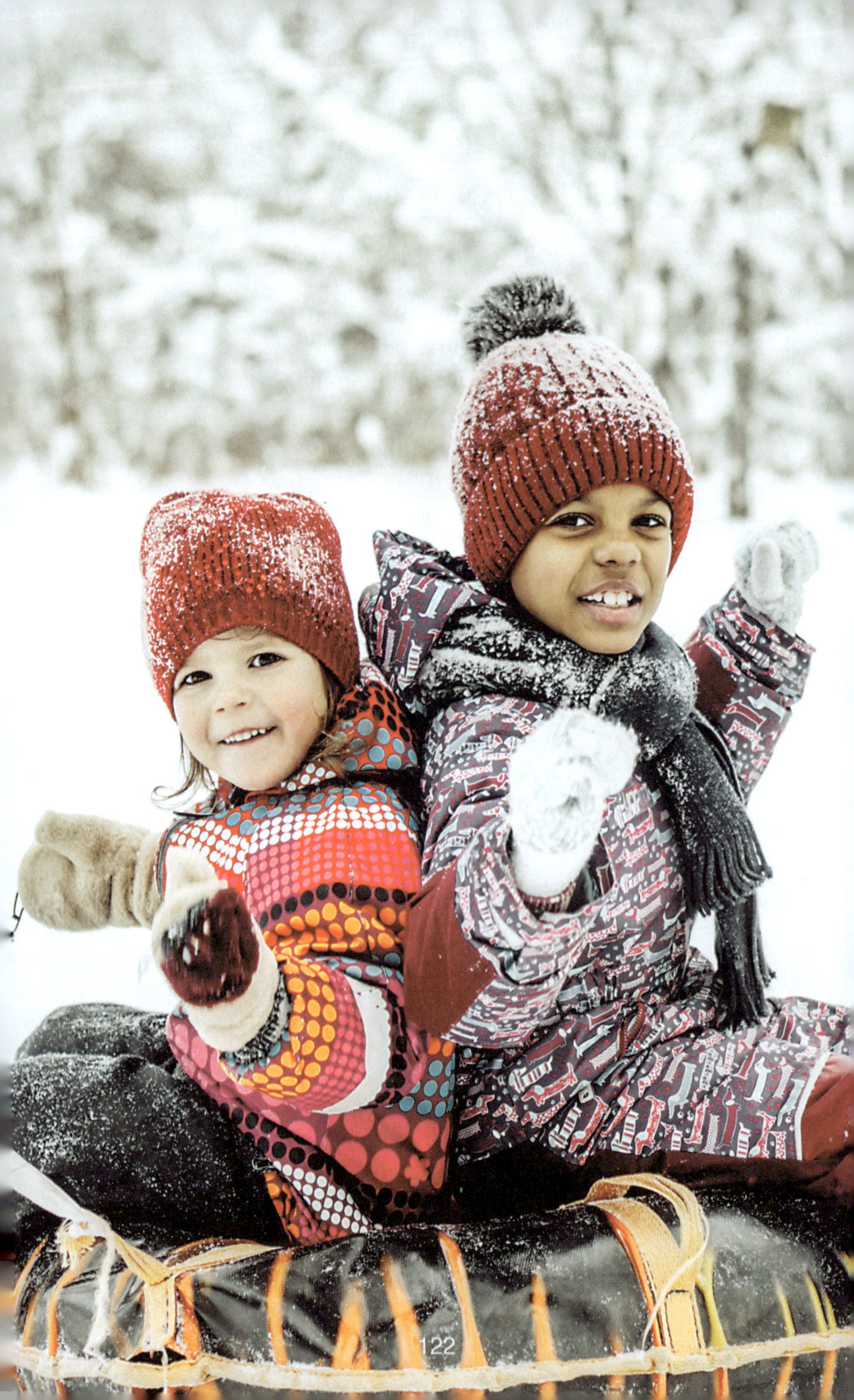

Wintertime Is a Time of Fun-Filled Magic

Winter may not seem like a season of magic
'Cause the air is so brisk and cold;
Sidewalks are icy and slippery,
And a blanket of snow unfolds.

Yet, it's still a magical season
If you view Winter with an open mind;
There's the sparkle of the new-fallen snowflakes
And so many priceless treasures to find.

Children anticipate joy and excitement
On a sled for two to share;
Mittens keep hands warm and comfy
As snowballs are tossed in the air.

Tall evergreens are powdered with white flakes,
And in the distance a bonfire glows;
Pheasants and turkeys strut freely
In a land they can now call their own.

The pond is frozen solid
And fills skaters with sweet melodies
As they twirl and swirl in circles,
Singing magical songs of glee!

Winter may not be as lovely
As the blossoms of Spring or a Summer's sun;
Yet, if you believe God can spin magic,
You'll discover Winter, too, is a season of fun!

Linda C. Grazulis

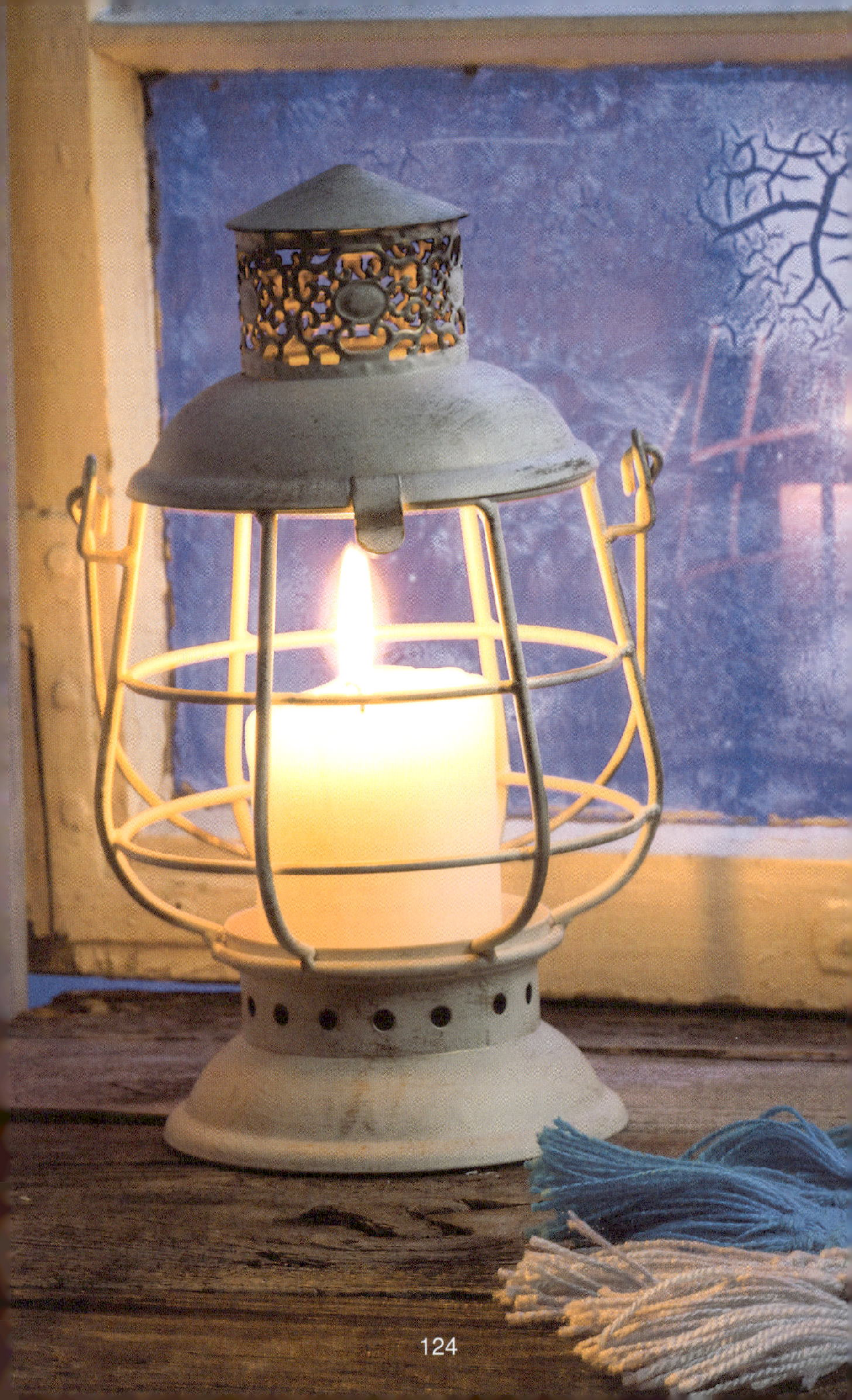

Altar Lamp

A world of white, fringed 'round with gray,
Are somber wood and snowy field,
'Neath sky that looks the same way.
All would an endless sameness yield
Except that edging silent stream
And splashed along the woodlot's edge,
Golden stalks of willow gleam
And briars of the wild rose wedge,
Like glowing jewels of ruby red.
How rich they look against the snow!
All dullness from the day has fled.
The fields are lit with lovely glow.
They are the lamp upon earth's altar
That says, there 'neath the snowy pall,
The gift of life will never falter.
It only waits for springtime's call.

Minnie Boyd Popish

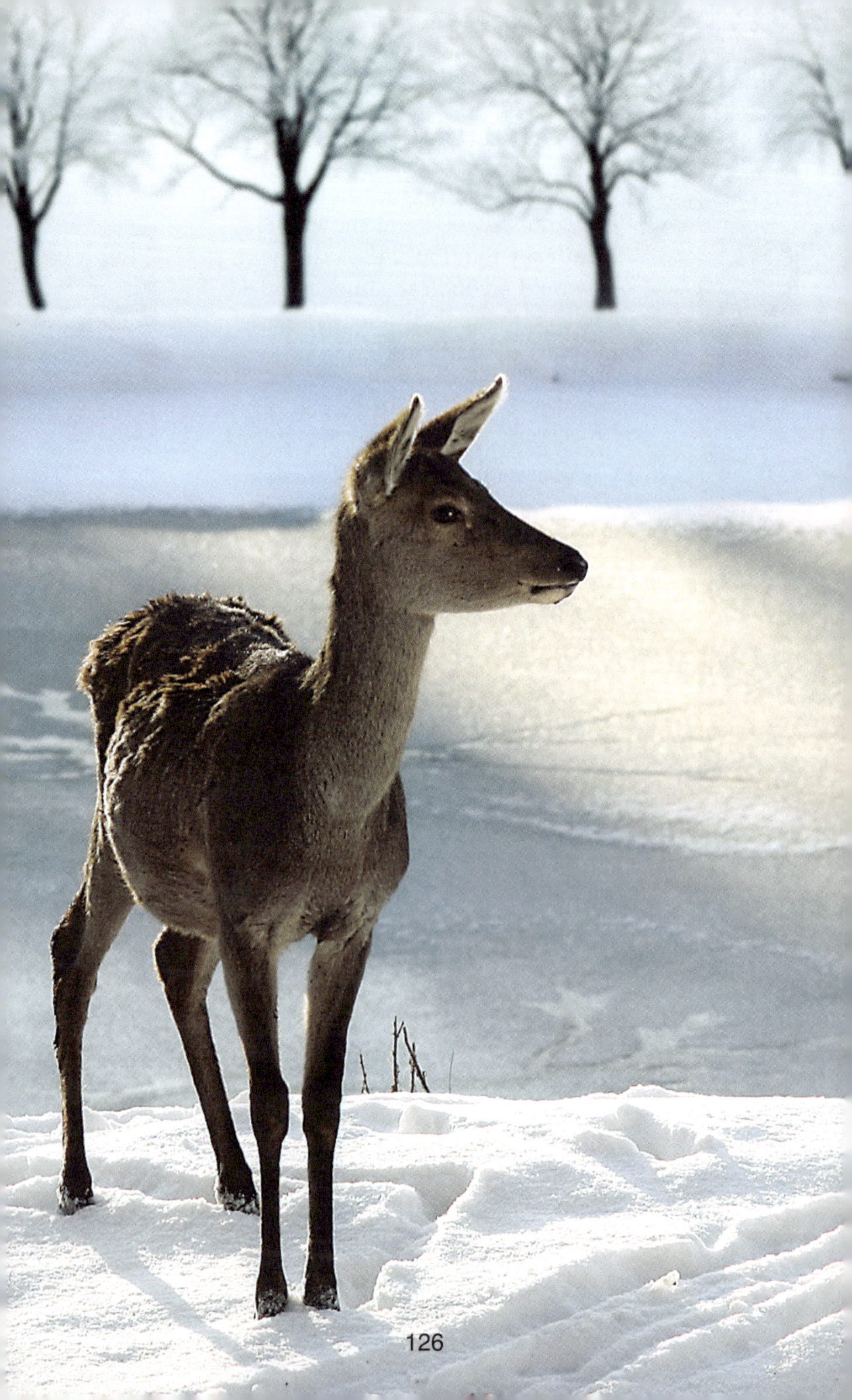

A World of White

A world of white today I greet;
Snow crystals crunch beneath my feet.
Trees wear sparkled, whipped-cream crowns
Atop their lacy snow-flaked gowns.

A world of white today I found;
Streams and rivers are ice-bound.
Birds have flown to southern climes,
And Winter's working overtime.

A world of white today was mine
In ice and snow and Winter-shine.
And though she sometimes is a fright,
Wintertime is pure delight.

Nora M. Bozeman

Winter

A cool sun shines down
On the naked trees
That seem to shiver
In the Winter breeze;
Then, icy winds
Sweep across the land
And clouds amass
So dark and grand –
An omen sure
This time of year
That very soon
The snow is near.

Viola P. Dickerson